TOPICAL GAS

A COLLECTION OF SHORT STORIES

BY

ROZ MALLINSON

Published by
Yfy Publications
86b Hammersmith Grove
London
W6 7HB
U.K.
Tel N: 020 8563 7370

CONTENTS

FOREWORD

This foreword is divided into two parts.

The first to the unsung hero of the literary world, the amateur writer.
The world is full of them, all busily scribbling away into the night, some never for money but for the love of writing. Some with hopes dreams and aspirations to see their work in print and others with grandiose ideas that this IS a best seller.

Amongst them lost from mainstream publishers are stars. One of them is called Ray Bessant. The first short story in this book is his, aptly named ' Murder in One Hundred Words.' It was written as a writing exercise and I came across it posted on a writer's site on the Internet.
It made my blood run cold!
Over the next few years, with Ray's permission, I have sent it to people all over the world, in Japan, India, Malaysia, Australia, Canada, South America, Israel, and the United States to name but a few, the reaction was always the same, 'Wow!'

Ray Bessant has given me permission to put his short story in this book and I am honoured to do so.

The second part of this foreword is dedicated to all the people who encouraged and helped me to achieve my hopes dreams and aspirations.
Every one has their muse and their mentors, some in unlikely places.
Here below are just a few of mine.

My thanks go to Samuel Flowers, who taught me to dream, and gave me courage.
To Mr Pryor who gave me sight and Mr Garland who gave me vision.
To Alice Laxton who never let me give up.
To my long suffering sons Peter and David Laxton who have had to hear every word, many times.
To June Nunn who in the midst of her busy life never forgets.
To friends Val and Brian Roberts - Maden who dare to dream as well.
Also to my granddaughters Gemini Louise Bayliss and Roxanne Louise Laxton without whose help and patience, my books would never make it into print.

MURDER IN ONE HUNDRED WORDS

The man sat on her bed.

She had opened her eyes and he was there..... as though he belonged.
He put a huge hand over her mouth to stifle her scream and said calmly,

'Every word you say brings you closer to death....I will rape and then kill you when you have spoken one hundred words.'

'Who are you? What do you want?' she croaked the words crawling tentatively through foul smelling fingers.

'Seven.' he said, tapping out the number of words on her throat with his little finger.

'This won't take long at all.' he said and smiled.

A MURDEROUS AFFAIR

The weekend at the residential home had been murder. The dishwasher packed up completely, and the washing machine sprang a leak. The staff were late changing shifts because of a rail strike, and some didn't bother turning in at all.

Mrs. Harris Jones refused to take her night medication and consequently roused the entire neighbourhood with her shouts of 'Fire! Fire!' at 2 a.m. Saturday morning, and 'Murder! Murder!' at 3 a.m. on Sunday. The other residents woken prematurely by the ensuing pandemonium were full of aches and pains and moans and groans. Confusion reigned when the chef was taken ill and the Agency cook couldn't find the street let alone the building.

By Monday morning everyone was thoroughly fed up. A staff member recounted the woes of the weekend to the new staff and commented,

'Its been sheer bloody murder here this weekend.'

With the release of tension began the germ of an idea. Everyone laughed and someone suggested a murder mystery weekend, and so began a chain of events that changed my life forever.

Bridget, a born organiser, soon had the venue and weekend chosen and people roped in. As with most staff events by the cut off date there was a distinct lack of interest but Bridget made up the numbers, as I knew she would. In a crisis her family were bullied into taking up the slack.

So on a cold windy Friday in October the chosen few departed in convoy from London, en route to the Birmingham Hilton where Inspector Riggs, ex - Birmingham CID held the 'Murder Inc' weekend for would-be sleuths.

The journey was smooth and quick and we arrived in time for lunch after which we decanted to our different rooms to await our first meeting with Inspector Riggs.

We were all roomed on the second floor of the west wing. Bridget and her husband Jim were in the room directly opposite me. On one side, her daughter Trish and Aunt Daphne, and on the other her niece Ann with her husband Bill. I had a single room across the corridor next to Bridget's adopted daughter Jane and her husband Paul. Both Bill and Paul were policemen and to be our aces in the hole when the going got tough.

Inspector Riggs turned out to be an excellent host and raconteur. Between Friday afternoon and Sunday lunch our group named Marple, alternately sleuthed for clues, interviewed witnesses, viewed the mock crime scene, read forensic reports and finally narrowed the suspects down to the two most likely actors.

We duly interrogated these suspects, using our two tame policemen shamelessly. As much of our delving over the weekend was accomplished in the bar, amid gales of laughter and numerous drinks, it was a very entertaining time and to be recommended as a stress beater.

Bridget's family welcomed me into their fold and I found myself warming to them. Jane was a tall statuesque blonde with a dry sense of humour and we exchanged nursing stories. Her husband Paul was very attentive, fetching drinks, moving chairs, opening doors etc. He was dark, athletic and very attractive.

Ann was the vibrant spark in the group, with flame red hair and cream skin much like myself. Bill seemed content to sit in her shadow, and smile enigmatically.

Daphne, Jim and Bridget were the jokers in the pack and regaled me with outrageous stories of Army life. Trish was quiet and sincere with an ethereal quality about her. Observing them all together it was easy to see how close knit they were as a family.

We finally chose our suspect and won our certificates for naming the said Jeffrey Finch as the perpetrator of the dastardly deed.

It was during the Sunday evening sortie in the bar that Jane and I found ourselves at the bar buying a celebratory round of drinks for the group and ordering snacks on the side.

Quite why Jane chose me or that moment to reveal what she did, I will never know. Maybe it was because I was the outsider in the group or because she'd had a few drinks, or maybe I had a friendly face and seemed a good listener.

'I think my husband is having an affair.' she blurted out.

I said nothing, waiting for her to enlarge or clam up.

'He's having an affair, I know he is, the bastard.' She repeated.

'Surely not.' I ventured with the caution of one entering a live minefield.

' Oh you think not.' She said bitterly. ' Acts the perfect husband doesn't he? But behind closed doors---. 'She left things unsaid.

'Are you sure?' I probed.

'Oh yes I'm sure.' She looked ready to cry and the last thing I needed was a scene so I tried to smooth things over.

'Perhaps you're reading too much into perfectly ordinary things.'

'He's been clever, very clever, well that's the policeman in him. Adept at covering tracks, but he can't fool me and this weekend has proved me right.'

'This weekend?' I faltered.

'Yes he brought his mistress with him.'

I remained silent.

'And I know who she is.' She hissed triumphantly.

'Who?' I thought frantically of any clues given away this weekend.

'Ann. Look at her sucking up to him now.'

'But she's with her husband.' I was in shock.

'Bill's always got his head on another planet. He wouldn't notice if she lay naked on the floor.'

I looked across the room to where Ann was coquettishly flirting with a very drunk Paul. He was obviously telling her something very funny and she threw her head back and laughed a beautiful tinkling laugh.

'Listen to the bitch.' Jane spat the words viciously.

'How can you be so sure its Ann?'

'I've watched Paul over the last few months, keeping tabs, opening his mail checking his clothes. I'm not a detective's wife for nothing.' She broke off as she saw my horrified expression.

'And?'

'I found lipstick on two of his shirts, Ann's colour, and I noticed perfume. That awful American perfume she buys through the shopping channel on cable T.V. you can't buy it anywhere else in this country.'

'But surely hundreds of women could have the same perfume and lipstick.' I protested.

'But not every woman writes notes to my husband arranging assignations.'

'An assignation?'

'Yes I found the note from her.'

'A note, when?'

'Today. It was pushed under the door this afternoon. When we were all supposed to go for a walk this afternoon, Paul cried off saying he was too tired and was going to read in the lounge. Ann said she needed to phone her children and make sure they were okay. I went back to our room for a warmer jacket and the note was pushed under the door whilst I was there. I read it and opened the door almost immediately, in time to see Ann slip into her room.'

I acknowledged it wouldn't take long to read the note.

The bartender finished making the snacks, and complete with drinks we carried the heavily laden trays back to the group.

'I'm sorry.' She said as we sat down together at a window sofa.

'Please don't say anything to anyone.'

'My lips are sealed.' I assured her, but I stayed close for the rest of the evening.

As hotel guests we were roped in by the staff to play quiz games made hilarious by the amount of alcohol being consumed until one by one we claimed exhaustion and retired to bed at one thirty in the morning.

I lay in bed listening to Jane and Paul having a heated row; although muted through the wall I could hear the anger in both voices.

I eventually fell into a deep sleep, the combination of exhilaration and drink consumed. It seemed only minutes later I was awakened by a shrill piercing bell ringing in my ears. I groggily turned on the bedside lamp, the clock said two thirty and an intermittent buzz was sounding every few seconds. The fire alarm!

I hastily pulled on slippers and robe and cautiously opened the door to find Bridget on the other side about to knock.

'Come on, its for real.' She said urgently.
'Have you knocked on Jane and Paul's' door?' I queried
'I've run along and knocked on all the doors in this corridor.'
Jim emerged from Daphne's room guiding her into the corridor. Trish followed with handbags and coats in her arms. Ann and Bill joined us and by now there were other people scurrying about so we hurried towards the main staircase. As we turned the corner I looked back and saw Jane and Paul coming out of their room. I waved but they didn't see, she seemed to be holding Paul up.
Too much alcohol I thought and then saw they were headed for another door marked fire escape, so I continued following the others.
Most of the guests in various forms of unsuitable night attire for the crisp October early hours, were gathered in the car park stamping their feet and swinging their arms in an attempt to keep warm. More and more people were arriving every second, and the night staff attempted some kind of roll call.
I kept looking for Jane and Paul but so far they had not put in an appearance.
Bridget also noticed their absence.
'I can't see Paul or Jane I hope they heard me knocking.'
'They were up, I saw them follow us down.'
We wandered through the crowd looking for them, leaving the others in Jim's car to keep warm.
Walking along the perimeter wall of the car park I

circumnavigated the lot but still saw no sign of the missing couple. I made my way back to Paul's car and when I approached I found Jane sitting in it, alone.

'Have you seen Paul?' she asked.

I had an inexplicable moment of dread.

'No, he isn't in the car park.'

'We got separated in the crush outside our room. I ended up coming down the main staircase I didn't see what happened to Paul. Why isn't he here?'

I looked at her, she was lying ! I had seen them go through the fire escape together.

Before I could pass comment Bridget and Jim arrived at the scene.

We conferred and Jim decided to speak to the night manager who had checked guests off as they arrived in the car park.

Paul was not on the list!

The senior fire officer was informed, and he ordered a thorough search to be made. Another officer made Jane repeat her story and she told the same lie she had told me.

My dread returned. Where was Paul, now was no time to play the fool, too much was at stake.

Jane became hysterical, Bridget tried calm words and soothing gestures but she became more manic. I watched the performance and couldn't help thinking the worse.

Some twenty minutes later the fire alarms silenced, a fireman explained there was a fault and the guests drifted slowly back to the hotel and their respective rooms.

Our group huddled together in the foyer waiting news of our missing member.

After an age the chief fire officer and the night manager approached Jim and took him to one side. They spoke in hushed whispers and Jim went off with them through the doors to the stairwell.

When he returned a few minutes later he was ashen.

He came and put his arms around Jane.

'Be brave love. They have found Paul.'

'Thank god. Is he hurt? Where is he?'

'There is no easy way to say this. Jane, he's dead.'

We all reacted with dismay.

'He was found at the bottom of the stairwell. It looks like he fell and broke his neck. A doctor and the police are on their way.'

'Police, why police?' I asked.

Jane made a keening sound, high and from the back of her throat, she looked dreadful. Her hands were shaking, and there was a fine film of perspiration on her face, tears coursed down her cheeks.

We found seats and staff brought us all a large brandy.

I gulped mine down in one shot. Jane sipped hers.

I was deep in thought, uppermost that Paul was dead and Jane was lying.

Much later the police and police surgeon took control of things but the preliminary findings were the same. Jim formally identified the body and the cause of death was a broken neck.

A policeman told us he wanted to ask a few questions about our movements the night before.

My interview was fairly quick.

He asked if Paul had had a lot to drink.

'Yes I'd agree with that we all had.'

'Did you see Mr and Mrs Carling after the fire alarm went off?'

'Yes, I saw Jane and Paul get separated by the crowd outside their room, Jane followed us down the main staircase and Paul went the other way.'

'How close were you when this happened?'

'About twenty, twenty five feet away, just as the corridor turns onto the main landing.'

'Did you see him after that.'

'No, I was in the car park and Jane joined us within a few minutes.'

That was it, the lie was told and the interview was over.

Other members of the group gave their statements saying more or less the same thing.

Preliminary investigations supported the theory that Paul had consumed a great deal of alcohol and fallen over the guard rail at the top of the fire escape, and the fall had broken his neck. There would be a formal inquest after a post mortem.

The doctor gave Jane an injection to calm her and hopefully help her sleep.

Bridget stayed with her awhile and as soon as I heard her finally retire to her own room I slid cautiously into the corridor. There was no one about. I tapped gently on Jane's door and went in. I closed the door quietly behind me. A pale and tearstained Jane was sitting up in bed. Had I been expected?

We looked at one another.

'How are you feeling now?' I asked.

'Numb. I loved him so much, I can't believe he's gone from my life forever.'

'It was an accident, he'd had too much to drink.'

'Yes but if only I'd held onto him.'

'Held on to him?' I queried.

She started and her face flushed.

'Outside the door.'

I nodded although I knew she meant something entirely different.

'There's no point in recrimination.' I countered, 'Try to sleep.'

'I can't.'

'Shall I make you some tea?'

'Would you that's very kind, my head is banging.'

'Perhaps a couple of painkillers would help?' I suggested.

'Please, I'm sure the injection will work in a while but something mild might help.'

I handed her two pills and she swallowed them with a little water from a glass on the bedside table. When the kettle boiled I made a cup of tea from the hotel hospitality pack.

'Would you like me to stay awhile?'

'Would you, I really don't want to be alone.'

'Of course, I'll stay until you are asleep.'

'I'm too upset to sleep.'

'Try to relax.'

'Easier said than done.' She hesitated, 'Did you mention our conversation to the police?'

'No, it was a private conversation, and not relevant.' I said carefully.

'At least she can't have him now.' She said bitterly.

'And neither can you!' I rejoined.

Her eyes met mine, and I knew beyond any doubt, I was looking into the eyes of a murderess.

She started to cry and I sat on the edge of the bed and put my arms around her.

Better to let her cry this out, and not betray any of the inner turmoil I felt inside.

'I'm sorry that was cruel.'

She continued to sob.

' Here let me get those painkillers for you.'

'I thought I'd just taken them.'

'No they're still on the table. Do you want a glass of water?'

'No thanks I'll take them with the tea.'

She put a pill in her mouth and sipped her tea and shuddered.

'God that's bitter.'

'Has it melted in your mouth?'

She nodded and said ruefully.

'I'm a nurse and I still can't take pills.'

'Can't take your own medicine.' I smiled and watched her closely. She took the second pill and shivered violently as she drank the tea.

'Is there anything else I can get you?'

'N no I'm fine, th... thank you.' Her speech was beginning to slur.

'How about a glass of water in case you wake, there's not much of the night left. If you sleep on in the morning I'm sure no one will mind.'

'Th.. thank you.' Her eyelids began to droop.

'Would you like two of your sleeping pills?'

Jane stared at me and I thought for a moment she was going to refuse, but she continued to stare at me with a rapt expression.

'Do you think I should?' she at last managed to say.

'I don't think it will do any harm at this stage of affairs.' I pointed to the bottle of sleeping pills, careful not to touch it now.

She picked it up her fingers uncoordinated and shook several pills onto the bed cover. She placed the bottle on the table and it fell on its side spewing pills onto the floor. She didn't notice, like an automaton she swallowed a few more, and then a few more.

I waited until she'd fallen asleep, then carefully washed out the dregs of drugs from the teacup and placed everything back neatly, then swiftly and silently checked the room before slipping next door where I waited.

The verdicts were accidental death on Paul and suicide while the balance of the mind was disturbed on Jane. Bridget blamed herself for leaving her alone and I comforted her as best I could under the circumstances.

I felt it was just deserts, for now I would never be with my beloved Paul. All the months of subterfuge and careful planning for nothing, because of a jealous wife, who had guessed the right motive but the wrong woman.

That weekend was to have been his last as a married man to Jane. Our long and passionate affair had blossomed into a loving mature relationship. He and I had been about to run away and start our new life together on the other side of the world.

We had tried to be kind and leave Jane in the loving care of her family at the hotel instead of at home when she was alone. Instead the murder weekend turned out to be a murderous affair.

ANOTHER DAY IN PARADISE

Today in this place in this town was Carlos' last chance. If he didn't succeed today then his life would change for the worse. It was at rock bottom now and he didn't know what worse meant in real terms only moved by the urgency of his elder brother's white face and whispered warning as Paulo had woken him at dawn.

'Please try again today carmacita, a little money will help.'

'I am tired.'

'Please Carlos, things will only get worse for all of us.'

He dragged himself from his cardboard shelf where his other brothers and sisters lay, found a pair of shorts and a dirty t-shirt and staggered out into the dawn.

He walked quickly to the town to keep warm and avoid the bandits that roamed the hills outside every town. He heard noises all round him as the forest came alive and fought the fear that rose within him as he remembered Pedro and what had happened to him. They had never found his body, only a few bleached bones a year later.

It was still bitterly cold even with the sun filtering light through the hills, it did not penetrate the dark narrow streets of the town.

Carlos chose his spot carefully. He was the first

child here today so maybe he would get lucky. The doorway made excellent cover with a deep step into the shadows. It was near enough to the market-square to make the frantic race but far enough from the police station to avoid the patrolling policemen outside.

Today he would stand as tall as he could and push aside all the other waving hands and bodies. He was ten years old and small for his age so sometimes the men looking for workers overlooked him and took the bigger children instead. But today he was desperate and he would do anything to attract the attention of the field boss.

In the café across the square Carlos could see the women making bread and smell the coffee. His stomach rumbled with hunger and his mouth salivated but he knew he must concentrate, watch for the first truck to pull into the market and be fast enough to run through the men watching and waiting just like him for a job any job to feed their starving families.

Carlos remembered when his father had driven just such a truck and come looking for workers. He and Paolo had sat in the front seats eating the warm panas Mamma had made for them and wondered what all the fuss was about. They had never worked in the fields then but watched other less fortunate children slave under the merciless sun to bring in the produce. As harvest after harvest had failed he and Paolo had helped his father eke out a living selling what little they managed to grow and when that too failed his father had spent most of his money in the local bars. His mother wept and found work in the local factory but this too closed and moved to the city.

When his father sold the farm they had put what they could on a cart and moved to his aunt's house, but his aunt and uncle died in a flu epidemic and their house was reclaimed by the rancher.

Eventually they found themselves in the Maratis ghetto living under galvanised roofing sheets and sleeping on cardboard. There was never enough food or water, they shared clothes and what they could scavenge.

One night he heard his mother and father screaming at one another and the next day a man had come and taken Paolo away. They did not see him for a long while and his father never spoke of him. Later Carlos had seen him drive past the market place in a big black car. He had new clothes and a new haircut but he looked very sad. When he turned to wave at Carlos he had a black eye and a cut lip. The man in the car pulled the blinds down. When Paulo returned home he had run away from the man and never spoke about his life although Carlos often heard him cry.

Suddenly there was a flurry of activity as three trucks kicking up dust came up the street to the Square. From every doorway and step, every ditch in the road , men and children swarmed, running to be first as the trucks screeched to a halt.

The dust settled and the throng moved forward,

Carlos weaving and ducking through the mass of arms and legs, jostling for a position at the front of the crowd. From the back of one truck a man wearing a red bandana climbed onto the roof of the cabin and surveyed the crowd. A mass of arms rose and cries of "Senor! Senor! Por Favor!" filled the Square. The man quickly pointed to men at the front of the crowd and a few children as well. They poured into the first truck which sped away out of the town. Then the next truck was filled, and went its way. Carlos jumped up as high as he could but a man snarled at him and pulled him to the ground and he was lost between a sea of legs. The last truck filled and drove off and the Square was quiet and deserted, men and children not chosen drifting into the shadows once more.

Carlos lay in the dirt tears in his eyes as he nursed his grazed knees. He needed to find work or money to day. Maybe he could become a bandit, join the men in the hills, maybe they would let him work for them. Or maybe if he made his way to the fields there might be work unaccounted for, he was strong, he would walk to the farm and ask.

He rose to his feet and walked quickly towards the edge of town passing men and women holding children in their arms, passing the Cafe where a few guards were gathered to have breakfast. Head held high he walked past the police station where a bored carbineri idly glanced his way before continuing to watch two others play boles in the dirt.

Soon he was out on the open road and his feet dragged through the dust. He was so hungry and now as the sun rose and beat down on him he was thirsty too. At the foot of the brooding hills, there was a stunted tree offering a little shade and Carlos made for it, he'd rest a little then head out for home again. He sat hunched over fighting hunger and thirst, his eyes drooping with tiredness, staring dreamily at an outcrop of rocks on the other side of the dusty road. As his sight adjusted to the heat haze he saw the outline of a man, standing very still, watching him. A bandit!! Carlos could see the rifle and ammunition slung round the mans chest. Carlos held his breath. What should he do? Run back to the town? Try to hide, or disappear into the hills and wait for dark? He was frozen with indecision.

The bandit continued to stare at him, motionless. He thought about the horrible tales he had heard about the fate people suffered at the hands of bandits especially children. In the distance he thought he heard the faint hum of an engine but try as he might he could not pull his eyes away from the man' s relentless stare.

Softly a big black car purred to a stop obstructing his view of the bandit. His dream like stare interrupted Carlos looked at the darkened windows on the car and inexplicably he shivered. This looked like the car Paulo used to drive round in. He stood up slowly as the back window slid down. A hand protruded through it and a hooked finger beckoned him to the side of the car.

Carlos hesitated and let his gaze wander over the car until he caught sight of the bandit again. The bandit shook his head slowly and motioned Carlos to cross the road. Carlos shivered and moved closer to the car, trying to see in. Maybe this was an offer of work or money, whatever it would save him from the bandits.

In a brief moment the car door opened and Carlos was hauled by his shirt into the back seat. He wriggled and squirmed but the hands holding him were strong. As Carlos struggled with one man he recognised the man sitting opposite as the man his brother had been with and cried out. The man was old, very old with a lined face and leaned upon a cane with a silver top.

'This one has spirit eh Joseph? ' the old man quavered.

'Like his brother Senor, but not for long. I won't make the same mistake twice.'

With a quick movement he tied Carlos' hands together and wrapped tape across his mouth.

Carlos struggled vainly to get out of the car but the old man beat his legs with the cane as the car moved off and gathered momentum. His last sight was of the bandit shaking his head as he turned and walked slowly back into the hills.

GOODYEAR'S LOT

'You advertised for a ghost writer?'
Brian Palmer stopped typing and turned in the direction of the voice.
'And you might be?'
'Jonathan Goodyear. You've heard of me?'
'No I can't say I have, but then I don't get out much.'
'Big mistake, you can lose touch with reality.'
'Yes I can see that, you're a ...?' Brian faltered with the question.
'A fairy.' Jonathan finished. 'What gave it away, the wings?'
'That and your height.'
Jonathan Goodyear raised himself to his full six inches and flapped his voluminous wings clearly annoyed.
' I don't believe in fairies and certainly not fairy writers.' said Brian.
'And why not? There is an annual fairy story in your writing magazine, an adult fairy story I might add.'
'You read The Millennium Writer?'
' Never fail, some interesting points of view.'
'And a copy is delivered to Fairyland I suppose.' said Brian sarcastically.
'Don't be silly. I read yours.' explained Jonathan patiently.' I thought we'd enter the fairy story competition this year, that's why I'm here.'

'I didn't advertise.'

'No you wished and here I am.'

'And just how would we collaborate on this venture?'

'Well I could give you inside information on what we eat, how we live, how we fly, where we go for our holidays, entertainment etc, nothing like accuracy to enhance a plot or,' he paused, 'I could write it for you.'

'Well that would help.'

'Of course it would help. You don't think Shakespeare wrote 'A Mid Summers Nights' Dream' without help do you?'

'Well,' started Brian.

'Or Tolkien wrote an entire middle earth language by himself.'

'That was you?'

'Yes that was me. We have decided that fairy writers have long gone unnoticed in this world and I have been sent to deal with the matter.'

'Why come to me? I've never had anything published.'

'Ah yes, you weren't our first choice. We had earmarked another writer but unfortunately it didn't work out. Told too many fairy stories in the human world and ended up in prison.'

'So how did you pick me?'

'I told you, you wished and here I am, and we were running short of time.'

'I seem to be suffering from writers block'

'Rubbish! Move over.'

Jonathan folded his wings, hovered above the keyboard and contemplated the computer screen. After a few moments he lowered himself gently onto the keys, hummed a few bars of 'Green sleeves' and began to dance.

Brian watched in amazement as Jonathan jigged and words jumped onto the screen. With every new song he sang he danced frenetically and page after page appeared. Finally he flapped his wings and flew onto the window- sill.

'Whew! I'm exhausted, but with a little judicious editing I think we might have a winner there.'

Brian peered at the screen, scrolling up then down then up again.

'Wow! ' He said.

'Give a fellow a drink.'

'Tea, coffee?' enquired Brian.

'Have you nothing stronger?'

Brian opened his solitary Christmas bottle of whiskey and looked around for a suitable receptacle. Jonathan unhooked a silver thimble from his back- pack and downed the proffered whiskey in one long loud gulp.

Over the next few hours Brian watched as Jonathan edited the story until it was concise, snappy, grabbed you in the right places and had a twist in the tale. When he was satisfied he added Jonathan Goodyear with a flourish.

'Don't you mean Brian Palmer.'

'Ah well no. You see you have all the fame and glory but in my name.'

'You didn't mention that.' retorted Brian.

'Did I mention you get to keep any monies accrued?'

'Err no.'

'You can pretend Jonathan Goodyear is a pseudonym, your nom de plume. Now how much is the entry fee?'

'Two pounds.'

Jonathan raked around in his pack again and came up with a pound coin, a dollar bill and a roman sestri. Brian looked in his wallet and found another one pound coin.

Brian was dispatched to the Post office to purchase the postal order and when he returned Jonathan was sleeping peacefully in the cat's hammock, having consumed the last of the whiskey.

Brian stared at the manuscript neatly stacked on the table. He addressed the A4 envelope and placed the manuscript inside. As he sealed the envelope he listened to Jonathan's gentle snores and thought about winning the competition and standing to receive his prize. In a moment he undid the envelope retyped the final page and with a furtive look over at the sleeping fairy signed his own name, then hastened out to catch the last post.

Jonathan opened one eye wearily, would mortals never learn to curb their egos, especially writers! To cross a fairy was very unwise, especially now with so much at stake. How could he go back to the newly formed Union of Fairy Writers or UFW and report failure?

The Queen of the Fairies had been adamant when they had complained of no recognition for centuries. Get one story published under your own name or be damned to ignominy for eternity, in fact no fairy writers ever again.

Of course Jonathan knew that the code of ethics for fairies required absolutely no interference without a mortal's acquiescence, so this was going to be tricky.

When Godfrey Bowman became a world renowned writer and then a politician he thought he had it made, instead of which the plot thickened to his downfall and he was stripped of rank and sent to jail. No never cross a fairy, it doesn't pay!

Jonathan winged his way back to Fairyland and joined his good friend Marmaduke Oldheart in The Queen Tit for a thimble of whiskey and a chat.

'You do see my problem?'

'Of course old man but what to do? You could cast a spell he did ask you in."

'Well technically' Jonathan blushed.

'Mmmmm.' said Marmaduke.

So the two of them drank well into the night and half the following day, there are no licensing laws in Fairyland because it's a twenty four hour job. The plotting and scheming went on and on, both rejecting plan after plan until Jonathan cried 'Eureka!'

'It's been done before.' sighed Marmaduke.

'No I've got it!' said Jonathan and laid out his plan.

Not many people know this but only female fairies

can change shape, something to do with multi tasking, so the plan involved sucking up to Alicia Lookinglass, yes she of Wonderland fame, and gaining her help.

Alicia was not in the best of moods. The previous day she had turned round quickly three times, thus divorcing her long suffering fourth husband Gordon Pikestaff, who was only too glad to be an ex and had skipped the toadstool taking the holiday money with him. The dating agency were being of no help, and had the temerity to suggest she was perhaps a trifle old and maybe she ought to hang on to husbands whilst she had them.

'You want me to do what?' she shrieked making both Jonathan and Marmaduke glad they were too old to be husband number five.

'We'll pay.' said Jonathan humbly, thinking of her depleted coffers.

'There will be no more fairy writers.' moaned Marmaduke, 'The Queen has issued a decree.'

'Stuff and nonsense.' said Alicia but then remembered her own poetry anthology lying dusty in a cupboard for lack of publication and thought better of it.

'Well it might work.' she muttered gloomily, 'But you Goodyear will pay handsomely and you Old heart will clean the cottage while I am away.'

'Cooeee Godfrey!'
Godfrey Bowman stopped in his tracks and wheeled round to face Alicia Lookinglass.

'Alicia darling, how are you.?' He planted the customary kisses on each cheek and pulled his overcoat closely round him.

'I'm as ever Godfrey, but you look wonderful, prison must have agreed with you.'

Godfrey looked anxiously round but they were quite alone. He had been bemoaning his lot to himself as he made his way through the King's Road Chelsea and wondering when he would ever be able to eat out again or buy any of the trendy goodies on sale when he heard Alicia's voice.

'What do you want Alicia?' he asked wearily.

'I'd like to try and make amends for the fiasco my friends caused you.'

'That's very big of you Alicia but didn't you have a hand in it somewhere?'

'Oh darling, lets not open old lesions. I'm here as a friend.'

'Ah yes a friend. you may have noticed Alicia I don't have many friends left'

Alicia grabbed his arm and said sweetly,

'All the more reason to treasure the ones you still have, lets have a drink and talk about your future.'

'I haven't got a future, you and your fairy friends saw to that. Neither have I home or job.' he muttered darkly.

Alicia pushed him through the doors of a trendy wine bar and manoeuvred him into a quiet corner booth. She ordered a good claret and then sat down opposite him , crossing her legs as provocatively as any Sharon Stone.

' Lets start putting things right. I may have just the job for you.'

'Robbing a bank? Mugging the P.M.?' he asked sarcastically.

'Godfrey behave! It was your own fault, you would meddle and then bend the truth.'

'If I bent it you positively crushed it into non recognition.'

The waiter arrived with their order uncorked. Alicia took the bottle and waved him away . She poured generous glassfuls of wine and sipped hers slowly. Godfrey downed his like a drowning man and poured another.

'This job you have?' he asked. 'Is it legal?'

'Not exactly illegal. I want you to judge a writing competition and we know who has won beforehand.'

'I thought so.' said Godfrey. 'That's how all my troubles started just doing a little favour for you.'

'Now Godfrey you know that isn't true. Had you kept your part of the bargain none of your woes would have overtaken you, but you crossed a fairy, several fairies in fact, and Queen Titania was adamant you pay the full penalty under the law.'

'Full penalty!' he spluttered. 'For stealing a few measly stories.'

'We aren't exactly responsible for your fairy tales in the real world or the long arm of the your law.'

'I lost everything, home, wife, family, money, job, and my reputation.'

'And now is the time to redeem yourself in our eyes

and who knows what will happen. What we have taken away can be restored.'

She swept her hand round , indicating the wine and food.

"Who is this job for?'

'The Millennium Writer.'

Godfrey raised his eyebrows and peered at her quizzically.

'Harry Smith's old rag. He'd never employ me. I had some rather unfavourable things to say about him and his magazine from the dock.' he said bitterly.

'Ah yes, but I think you'll find he's desperate, so all might be forgiven, but I warn you Godfrey if you meddle again....' she left the threat hanging in the air and Godfrey shuddered.

'And pray tell how am I to become this judge, by telepathy ?'

'Well I think Harry should be along any minute. He'll be surprised to see you but I'll explain we are old friends .'

'He knows you?'

'Intimately.' she smiled knowingly.

The door of the wine bar opened and a harassed Harry Smith stepped through looking confused.

Alicia sidled over to him.

'Hello Harry .' she said breathlessly.

'Darling .' he spluttered equally breathless.

'We are over here in the corner away from prying eyes.' she blinked her large blue eyes and ran her fingers over his hand.

'And I have brought a friend who might be the

answer to all your problems.' she cooed.

Harry Smith and Godfrey Bowman eyed one another coolly.

'Godfrey.' said Harry curtly.

'Harry.' responded Godfrey.

Neither proffered a hand.

"How are you?' asked Harry.

'Fine .' said Godfrey, 'And your good self?'

'Mustn't grumble.'

Another bottle of wonderfully rare and expensive claret appeared on the table.

'And the magazine?'

'As popular as ever.'

'I was just telling Godfrey about your run of bad luck.' Alicia interceded.

Harry patted her knee solicitously,

' We don't need to be worrying Godfrey about that, I'm sure he has more pressing matters to deal with.'

Harry eyed the door and then Godfrey meaningfully.

'Well I am somewhat of an expert on bad luck Harry, as you may have noted of late.'

' It might help Harry if you explained the difficulties you are having.' prompted Alicia.

Harry glared at her, Godfrey feigned disinterest, and she tucked her arm into Harry's.

'Please, just for me.' she begged.

'Oh alright, but what good it will do.'

Harry leaned forward conspiratorially.

'You know about my magazine, it relies heavily on advertising and until now mainly small businesses.'

Godfrey nodded.

'Every year we run annual competitions, another source of income, one of which is the Annual Adult Fairy Story.'

'Yes I think Alicia has mentioned it.' said Godfrey dryly.

'So imagine my surprise when a major, and I do mean major pharmaceutical company, approached me wanting to launch a new product and advertising campaign, linked to the competition.'

'Ah. Big bucks all round.'

Exactly!'

'So what's the problem?'

' Every damn judge I get to adjudicate and present the prizes, big ones I might add, runs out on me after a few days. The fifth one pulled out this morning.'

'Five?' Godfrey eyed Alicia suspiciously.

Harry held up a podgy hand and counted on his fingers.

'One, a film script in Hollywood. Two is personally interviewing the Dalai Lama somewhere in the Himalayas, three had an unexpected legacy in the form of a boat and sailed to the Caribbean, four found God and has gone off to a monastery, and five has fallen in love and just has to meet her parents in Papua New Guinea.' He sat back and rolled his eyes.

'I give up! Its doomed before I get it off the ground.'

Alicia studied her long blood red nails and nudged Godfrey under the table.

'Well maybe not.' he faltered.

Harry looked right through him.

'I mean I could do it. I have history sure, but before all this nightmare began I was a fairly well respected author.'

'And beloved by the competition circuit.' cut in Alicia.

'I don't know if the Gallico Corporation would wear that.' said Harry.

'Rubbish!' said Alicia, 'It will be more publicity for you, the magazine, the product, the company and Godfrey.'

'They rely on a squeaky clean image.'

'Then imagine the headlines.' Alicia spread her hands in the air as if reading ten foot high letters.

'Author cleaned up act with the aid of Wand and the Gallico Corporation.

Both men turned to look at her.

'Well it might work.' said Harry begrudgingly.

The concert hall was packed, it seemed that any one who was anybody was there. Harry Smith was pleased with the choice of venue, much larger than he would have chosen but it had paid off. Journalists and honoured guests, the Gallico directorate en masse and with entourage, competitors and friends, and 'Alicia's idea' ticket holders. Ticket sales had gone through the roof for what was normally a mediocre attendance at best.

Godfrey had been introduced to the directors of the Gallico Corporation over a dinner party hosted by

Alicia and he had been a great success. Harry had to admit he was a great after dinner raconteur.

Alicia was looking splendid in a sheath dress of gold satin fabric that clung in all the right places and was doing what she did best, being an excellent hostess, whilst Godfrey smooth and sophisticated in his tuxedo was mixing with the crowd, who certainly seemed excited and enthralled to see him.

Up in the great domed ceiling tucked behind two frolicking cherubs Jonathan and Marmaduke watched as Alicia touched Godfrey's arm and he turned and smiled at her, and they moved on through the crowd.

'You don't think.....?' Marmaduke let the question hover .

'No! Not in a millions years.'

'She can shape change.'

'Yes but she can only stay human with Queen Tit's permission.'

'Queen Tit is awfully fond of her, and she is looking for husband number five.' Marmaduke mumured.

Jonathan peered down through the gloom watching Alicia as she fawned over Godfrey.

'Oh my! She'd lead him a merry dance.'

"Yes, but not in our world.'

They both chuckled.

Down in the auditorium Brian Palmer sat with clenched sweaty hands. When he'd first been short listed he'd been shocked. Then when it was down to the last five he became alarmed. Until then he hadn't given the fairy a thought but supposing he won. Would things go smoothly or would that blasted fairy interfere. The prize was ten thousand pounds and what he could do with that money!.

He looked round anxiously, not a fairy in sight.

'Are you short listed young man?' asked an elderly lady sat next to him.

'Yes I am.' he faltered.

'Good luck.' said Queen Titania.

The evening wore on with various acts interspersed with commentary by Godfrey.

Then it was time for the prize giving which went smoothly.

'And now we come to the final prize for the Adult Fairy Story."

Godfrey made a great ploy of opening the large gold envelope.

'It is with great pleasure I award this prize from the Gallico Corporation makers of Wand Soap Powder to.....'

Brian held his breath.

'Jonathan Goodyear.'

The audience clapped and cheered for a few minutes but Brian stayed rooted in his seat.

'Jonathan Goodyear.' repeated Godfrey looking round.'

Jonathan and Marmaduke hung from the cherubs their wings aquiver looking for the bogus author.

Alicia scanned the audience smiling.

Queen Titania took Brian firmly by the arm with a 'That's you dear isn't it.' and propelled him firmly through the seats to the stage. Brian thought he saw a flurry of wings but couldn't be sure as Godfrey received him enthusiastically. He leaned into the microphone.

'Sometimes we forget our own pseudonyms. I started life as Cedric Higginbottom so you see why I clearly use Godfrey Bowman.'

The audience tittered but Alicia pricked up her ears, she'd never had a Cedric before.

Brian looked at the manuscript thrust into his hand and sure enough it was signed Jonathan Goodyear as was the large cheque held out to him.

He felt faint. Just when had Jonathan Goodyear altered the name? He searched the faces on the stage and thought he recognised the blonde girl from the submissions office and then Godfrey winked at him.

Queen Titania shoved a piece of paper at him and hissed 'Acceptance speech.' and Godfrey led him to the dais and adjusted the microphone.

He muttered the banal platitudes and then graciously accepted the cheque, his mind reeling.

Queen Titania helped him back to his seat.

'Now young man how simple was that, exchanging your writer's ego for a fortune. I take it we understand one another now.'

'You're a ...

'I am Titania, Queen of all the fairies, and I trust you have learned a valuable lesson.'

'How will I get the money?'

'Oh I am sure your luck is about to change, for the better.' she pronounced.

Brian smiled wanly. Various members of the public shook his hand, and congratulated him.

Harry approached with a distinguished looking man in tow.

'Well done young man.'

'Thank you. I am a little overwhelmed.'

'Allow me to introduce Maxwell Schell.'

'The Maxwell Schell! The publisher?'

'The very same... My card. Give me a ring.'

Queen Titania smiled

'We will.' she said as he walked away.

'You see.' she said to Brian,' For helping a fairy you get rewarded for crossing one you get...' she pointed to Alicia hanging on Godfrey Bowman's arm,' A difficult lady to please I'm told.'

Brian watched in amazement as Godfrey Bowman kissed the blonde girl.

Harry looked on in amusement.

He thought back twenty years to when he had first met Queen Titania. She had approached him with great sadness.

'Our world is dying and because of the constraints of our species it will be left to the female fairies to carry on. We need a way to integrate the two worlds, to introduce fairies into a world that no longer believes or wants them.'

And so the Adult Fairy writing competition had been born. With financing from the fairy coffers Harry's small but very profitable empire had grown.

'No Godfrey,' he thought, 'It doesn't do to cross a

fairy especially the female of the species.'
The auditorium was almost empty now. She summoned Jonathan and Marmaduke and they flew down and nestled in her handbag.

She looked down at them.

' Well done! Consider the Union of Fairy Writers well and truly inaugurated.'

COMING HOME

The boy lay in the ditch his head level with the
road. He could feel the coarse wet ground beneath
him as his hands clenched and unclenched with
each wave of pain. If he turned his head just a little
he could see the farmhouse so clearly, just ten
yards away, just beyond his reach...home.

He turned his gaze concentrating on the sky. The
gravid moon hung low and the stars were losing
their brightness as dawn approached. Maybe if he
looked hard enough he would be able to see the
North star, then he could make a wish. Oh how he
wished he could be home tucked up in his soft bed
far away from all this, way before the nightmare
began. The pain was harsh now and his head reeled
from the blinding flashes behind his eyes. A solitary
tear escaped and mingled with the blood on his
face. He tried to call out but no sound came.
Keep still an inner voice warned him, writhing about
will only make it worse. As if anything could be
worse, forget the beating his whole world had
collapsed around him and would collapse around
others and he had no way to warn them, to let
them know his temper had betrayed him yet again
but this time with consequences for the others in
his life, the two people that mattered most to him,
his sister and grandmother.

He remembered vividly the day he and his sister had come to live with Nana.

They had stood bleary eyed and tearful at her door after their long ride from the city, not really understanding the black clothes and holes in the ground where their parents lay. The door had opened light streaming towards them and in the light a soft voice reached out through their fear and grief.

' Come in children and warm yourselves by the fire.' Two large strong floury hands held theirs and led them into a big kitchen. How wonderful the smells from the large oven, how bright the fire, how loving those arms were. Throughout their childhood the kitchen had been the heart of the home provided by Nana and her love had been so encompassing he had never thought the outside world could touch them there.

But how soon it had. Schooldays for him had flown by and here he was waiting to go to University, his sister leaving school and becoming a beautiful young woman, turning heads wherever she went. Nana was so proud of them and never missed an opportunity to tell all and sundry about her two beautiful grandchildren.

When had he first noticed the change in his little sister? he couldn't say or pinpoint a moment the alteration had been so gradual. Late home from school, long walks alone, furtive phone calls, dropping her friends. Nana had said it was part of growing up and kept a close eye on her. Had he not been so close to his sister maybe he would not have noticed the difference, but she had drawn apart from him and he had suffered in her rejection. She had always been the popular child with many friends and invitations and he the loner always with his head in a book. They were so unalike, chalk and cheese, as Nana said, but they had each other and had shared hopes dreams and aspirations. He lost touch a little while he studied for his entrance exams, maybe that's when it had happened.

One night a car had dropped her on the corner of the street, not outside the door, which was unusual. He had stood and stretched after a few hours at the computer, casually looking out the window he had seen the drop off and teased her gently the following morning. Eyes blazing she had told him to mind his own business and stormed out slamming the door behind her.

'It's a boy.' said Nana and he had been startled into realising his baby sister was turning into a woman more quickly than he realised. So he had made up his mind to find out who the boy was but his sister had guarded the secret well and it was only a chance sighting when he was on a field trip one day. He left a museum and glanced up to see her in a coffee house. He had half lifted his hand in greeting but stopped as she had smiled sweetly up at a man who sat down at her table. An older man, much older with grey in his hair and a care worn face. He watched as they talked animatedly, the

man occasionally reaching out to touch a strand of her hair or caress her hand.

Later that evening he had confronted her but she had refused to discuss the matter with him. He had begged and pleaded with her to end the affair and she had laughed at him told him she had no idea what he was talking about.
'I saw you!'
'Then if you know what's good for you you'll forget what you saw.' she hissed.
'He's old enough to be your father, no correction grandfather.' he spat back.
'That's a good enough reason for me not to be having an affair with him .'
'Then why meet him? Why all the subterfuge?'
'Forget what you saw, for your own sake forget.'
But he couldn't and he hadn't. He had watched and followed her, neglected everything in his quest to discover the truth and end the liaison between his sister and the man. They had certainly kept a low profile and weeks had stretched into months before he saw them together again. They had met on a crowded street, no words were exchanged the man just handed her a package. It was quick, just a sleight of hand that had he not been watching would have been lost to the casual observer, but when she turned away her eyes shone, her face was radiant and there was a lightness in her step. This time he followed the man. Not a straight

forward exercise, it was if the man knew he was being followed, for he twisted and turned through the streets of the city until eventually he was lost on the outskirts of the city.

One minute the man was in sight the next he was gone, not even a door closing to show where he had disappeared. Though he had waited for hours the man never reappeared, and disappointed he had returned home dejected and worried.

For the next few days no one moved very far from home as there had been another bombing and Nana was frightened for them. It had been school and then home while the army patrols stopped every car and truck along the main road into the city, everything slowed, everyone held their breath.

Two weeks later life had returned to some normality and he decided the only way to know more about the man was to tail his sister. Easier said than done as she seemed to have a sixth sense whenever he planned to follow her and did her best to conspire to keep him out of the frame. But one night he borrowed a friends car and he managed to just keep her in sight. He had by now decided the man must be married and her behaviour only served to enforce that idea. She too doubled back on her tracks, taking side roads and criss-crossing roads she walked down until he was dizzy.

Finally she knocked on the door of a house in what looked like a deserted street, no cars no people, no movement, and disappeared inside. He was confused, this was nowhere near the area he had lost the man before.

What should he do, knock on the door, storm in, what? After a few minutes his sister came out carrying another package, an arm shot out of the doorway, spinning her round and she laughing pushed the arm away and ran down the street.

He was out of the car and across the street before she had turned the corner. He ran straight at the door his heart pounding and burst the door open with his shoulder. He just had time to register the look of shocked surprise on the faces of the four men sat round a table, the clocks, the wires the guns, before he was pistol whipped.

When he regained his senses he wished he hadn't. He was bound to a chair with duct tape his hands cable tied behind him at an impossible angle.

His head throbbed and he felt blood welling in his mouth and throat. He was alone with the man, the others had gone. The man pulled his chair up close to him and leaned into him, face to face his eyes boring into his.

'Not a sound boy.' he whispered.

He tapped him on his knee and the pain shot up through his body like a red hot poker, he tried to scream but no sound came out not that he could hear. He waited for the pain to subside and through tear filled eyes looked down at his knees and then he did scream at the bloody mess.

There followed the worst few hours of his short life, while the man alternately questioned him or inflicted pain as he drifted in and out of consciousness. When the man knew who he was and the whole story of the affair he had laughed. A cold quiet laugh that made the boy shudder.

'Your sister and I had a business arrangement. She carried packages for me and I paid her well.'

'She wouldn't.'

' Oh but she did.' the man smiled.' She couldn't wait to leave the stifling life on the farm and money was her only way out, but now....'

The unspoken words sent a chill through the boy as he realised the use of the past tense. In a moment he realised not only had he endangered his life but also the lives of his sister and grandmother.

'Please don't hurt them.' he managed just before a blinding flash took him back to oblivion.

When he woke he was in a car travelling fast and with each bounce the agony in his body increased. He choked on his own vomit tears and blood. When the car stopped he was hauled out unceremoniously and dumped into the ditch and as he was thrown he saw the farmhouse so near yet so far. Home!!

The car drove off, all was silent. The man hadn't gone to the house, it was over, though his life was forfeit the man had not gone to the house.

Maybe his sister would be safe, she wouldn't talk, of that he was sure. Maybe she hadn't outlived her usefulness, and his grandmother who knew nothing.

As life slowly ebbed from his battered body a light came on the kitchen flooding the strip of land between window and ditch, shining across the road like a beacon. He smiled, they were safe!!

A dark shadow crossed the window as the man cocked his gun and silently mounted the stairs.

FEEDING PIRANHA

'Oi you! If you ain't gonna buy that stop mucking it
abaht.'
June railed at a young man rooting through the
paraphernalia on her stall and throwing things on
the ground.
'That's all good gear that is.'
The youth gave her a friendly smile and held up a
pair of jeans.
'How much?' he said.
'A pound to others but fifty pee to you 'cos you
smiled.'
'Done.' he said and stuffed them into his carrier bag
and handed her the money.
The Saturday morning Boot Sale was in full swing
and packed with people milling from stall to stall.
June and her friends had three good stalls near
the only entrance and exit. They had met ten years
earlier when Boot Sales were just starting up and
through all kinds of weather had turned out
regularly for this one held in the old church
grounds. They were firm friends and supported one
another through the good and bad times.
A gaggle of teenage girls jostling one another
mobbed Iris' stall.
'You got any Ice Frosted Peach Drop by Revlon?'
said one of the girls.

'Darlin' there must be five 'undred lippies in that box, I ain't tried everyone.'
The other girls did an impression of bored while she looked.
'Well I'll have this one then.'
'Twenty pee.'
'Ta.' the girls moved on.
'I got a load of old tat this week.' moaned June.
'You got a load of old tat every week' laughed Iris and May.
A big black woman pushed her trolley to the stall.
'What size are these curtains?'
'That size.' said June pointedly. 'Dunno darlin' 'ave a measure.' and handed the woman a tape measure. The woman deftly took measurements.
'They'd fit my back bedroom lovely.' she said.
'A tenner.' said June.
'Fiver.' said the woman swiftly.
'Nine.'
'Six.'
'Eight and that's my final offer.'
'Done.' Money given, curtains taken the woman was on her way again.
'Them was lovely curtains, came out of an 'otel in the Strand.' said June.
'You can always tell good curtains , lined and weighted.' agreed May.
'You can't get the lead weights any more.'
'When I make mine I use fifty pence coins in the corners.' said Iris.

'Fifty p!' exploded June.' You made of bleedin' money? Three two p coins do exactly the same.'
A bevy of heavily veiled women flooded through the gates.
'Oh ' ere they come girls.' remarked June. 'Get ready to sell your souls.'
'Dunno how they could wear that rigout in this heat.' said Iris.
'Well it's 'ot were they come from 'innit.' said June.
'Its something to do with their religion.' said May.
'What's religious about that?'
'Allah decreed no other man save there husband should look upon their beauty.'
'No man should see if they're bleedin' ugly you mean.' laughed June.
The women picked through the boxes of goods on the three stalls. They grabbed armfuls of clothes and gesticulated with their fingers what they wanted to pay.
'Oi! Wot you think this is a bleedin' charity. You want all that lot its a fiver to you and a tenner to you.' said June pointing to two women heavily laden. They bought and moved on.
'What do they do with it all?' wondered June
'Dunno.' said the other women.
'Maybe there's a black market in tat.' they all laughed.
A girl approached Iris with a jar.
'Is this anti ageing cream?'
'You don't need that darlin' you're far too young.'

'Nah its for me Mum, it's her birthday.'

May and Iris exchanged knowing looks.

'Sweetie, trust me on this, as a daughter never give your Mum anti-ageing cream.'

'It's what she asked for.'

'Then darlin' let some other mug buy it for her. Here I've got some lovely perfume, the real McCoy!.'

'Knocked off is it?' chirped the girl

'Cheeky!' Iris winked and handed the girl a beautiful gift box packed with goodies.

'That's twelve pounds or I got a smaller one at six.'

'I only got a tenner.' wailed the girl.

'Oh go on then seeing as its your Mum's birthday.'

'Oh thanks.'

The girl carefully put the box in her shopping bag and went off.

'Me bleedin' feet are killing me.' moaned May.

'Take the weight off girl then, 'ere's a stool.'

May perched on a fold up stool and stretched her legs in front of her.

"Ere look at me plates of meat.'

Iris and June looked sympathetically at her swollen feet.

'You taking them pills the doctor gave you?'

'Yer, religiously.' May winked. ' As if Ray would let me forget! 'Ere do you like me earrings?' she swung her head revealing large hooped earrings studded with diamonds and sapphires.'

'You won the lottery?' laughed June

'In a way. Ray bought them for me when the doctor

gave me the all clear.'
'So no more treatment?'
'Nah the cancer's all gone, me mouth is clear.'
'Well thank the Lord for that after all that worry.'
'I did think I'd 'ad me chips.' said May.
'Talking of food any one want a tea?' asked June
'Ooh ta love, me throats gagging.' said Iris.
'Fancy a bacon sarnie?'
'Yes please.'
June purchased three teas and three bacon baps
from the burger stall and they all munched happily,
taking turns to serve small waves of customers.
The boot sale stalls sprawled as far as the eyes
could see and Saturday morning always brought a
good crowd, traders early, regulars next, and then
the odd wayfarer pulled in by the lull of a bargain or
two. At fifty pence it was a good mornings
entertainment, and ten per cent of the profits went
to the church.
The smell of frying onions and burger fat lay in the
air and June watched two little boys playing in the
dusty earth in the church gardens.
'Them kids have been there all morning.' she said.
'I know, they must be thirsty poor little fellas.' said
May.
'Give us me purse, I'll get them a drink.'
June purchased two cokes from the hot dog stand
and picked her way through the stalls to where the
boys were engrossed in lining up stones.
'Hello.' she said.
Two pairs of solemn brown eyes surveyed her, but

no smile just a general wariness.

She held out the cans to the boys. The smallest raised his hand but the bigger boy knocked it away. They looked down at the ground.

"Ere you are then.' she placed the cans on the ground near them and walked away. After a short distance she turned back and watched them drink thirstily.

She smiled and went to the stall and got two packets of crisps. She returned and threw them on the ground next to the boys. They looked up at her, still unsmiling.

'Forgot your manners, don't say ta.' she said

The boys tore open the crisps and ate greedily, then the little one smiled, a gap toothed crooked grin that melted her heart.

She returned to the stall.

'Anyone seen anybody with them?' she asked generally of the stall holders, but no one had.

It was a hot day so they took it in turns to sit in the shade, or fetch cool drinks, but by three pm when they were starting to pack their wares away, still no one had approached the boys, they still played in the dust.

'Look like little angels.' said May.

'Angels with dirty faces and empty bellies.' said June. 'I wonder if they will eat a burger?'

'Well you could try.' ventured May.

The burger stall was also packing up, two burgers and two more cokes were duly purchased and June took them to the two boys. They snatched them

from her hand and set to eating them quickly and
slaking their thirst.
'Is your Mommy here?'
The boys looked up blankly.
'Mum, Mama.' she repeated.
The eldest pointed out to the street.
June looked up and down the road but there was no
woman in sight.
She watched as they finished the food and drink
and then held out her hands.
'Come on boys, you're coming with me.'
They held on to her hands tightly as she took them
back to the stall.
'Blimey they for sale?' laughed Iris.
'No but if they stay here alone they might be.' said
June thoughts of lurid media coverage of
paedophiles and murder foremost in her mind.
'It only takes a minute for a pervert to strike.'
The other women nodded their heads, they too had
grandchildren and worried for them.
'No sign of the mother then?'
'No but if she is around we are in a good position so
we will see her.'
Iris tossed June a pack of baby wipes from the front
of her stall.
'They could do with a rub down.' she laughed.
June quickly wiped the protesting boys faces and
hands and bundled them behind her stall so they
could sit on the tail gate of her car.
By now the public had gone and the traders were
leaving the grounds in their cars and vans. Soon

only June, Iris, May and the boot sale manager
were left. Even the hot dog stall had disappeared.
'You two go on I'll hang around another twenty
minutes, if no one shows I'll phone the law.' said
June. Iris and May closed their car doors and with
waves pulled out of the grounds. June parked her
car outside in the street while the manager locked
the gates.
'Well any ideas where your mother is boys?' June
asked them.
They shook their heads solemnly.
'Do you even understand what I'm saying?' she
muttered.
They sat in silence for about ten minutes. Each
moment June thought of all the things she should
be doing at home and how long it would take if she
had to take the boys to the police station and
maybe make a statement.
For her there were never enough hours in the day
as it was she had so many family commitments. She
looked anxiously around, this was not a good
neighbourhood to sit around in, car or not. She
glanced at her watch and then into her driving
mirror at the boys seated behind. She saw them
stiffen and grow wide eyed and followed the
direction of their eyes. A tall black man had turned
into the road and was walking towards the car,
swinging his hips and dreadlocks as he sang in time
to a walkman clipped on his belt.
'Do you know him?' she asked the boys.

They didn't speak but it was obvious they did from their body language.

She honked her car horn and the man looked up took a few more faltering steps towards the car then turned and legged it, running across the road, jumping a small wall and racing into the park.

'Stay here.' she said to the boys and jumped out of the car and followed the man. June in her youth had been no mean athlete but when she reached the other side of the park the man was nowhere to be seen.

Damn she thought, now what and retraced her steps.

As she approached her car she could see no sign of the boys and with a sinking feeling she got in. Her handbag containing her wallet, credit cards, shopping money, her diamond rings that she always removed for safety and the days takings were gone! As were the boys. She ruefully estimated the loss, five hundred pounds in money, the rings were two or three thousand pounds, then thought of the long night ahead of her cancelling credit and bank cards, and reached for her mobile phone to ring the police. That had gone as well! Her house keys were in her bag and damn a bill with an address on.

She quickly put the car into gear and raced for home, praying that Ray was in and no further losses would be incurred. What a fool and what a scam. Two lost little innocents my foot, I've just fed and watered piranha!!

LOVE LIES WAITING

Phyllis Simpson loved her home.

Situated in a quiet London side road, on the top floor of a converted Victorian house, with inaccessible balconies and anonymous neighbours, she lavished affection and money on the flat, the bright spot in her otherwise dull existence and her love showed. The apartment shone after a recent refurbishment, and she'd added a few pieces of antique furniture exhausting her budget, but felt the expense had been worth it, her home had an air of opulence and she was happy.

She relaxed in her favourite armchair listening to a classical recording on the radio and admired the soft glows from the walls and the pristine white doors.

During one of these loving glances she saw the face, it materialised at the entrance door. She turned on the overhead light, her heart racing. It was still there, a face or the illusion of it, amongst the jumble of security locks recently installed after a spate of local burglaries. She approached the door laughing at her fears; of course there was nothing there. Fascinated she ran her fingers down the door looking for a blemish but the wood was completely smooth, but when she returned to her seat the face reappeared. She studied the large open mouth, the two half-closed eyes and the long aquiline nose; it seemed to be laughing. Miss Simpson was used to solitary living and was far too sensible to be frightened but it disturbed her sense of order. She resolved to phone the decorator first thing in the morning.

Mr. Morris was most obliging and assured Miss Simpson he would put things right, and on the following Monday as she set off for work he arrived and amid much fuss about dust sheets and cup rings, he sanded and repainted the front door. That night she settled in her favourite armchair with a meal for one and an episode of Morse on the T.V.

In a commercial break and when she least expected it the face returned still smiling. She was dismayed and blinked several times, but the face stayed, complete with smile.

Mr. Morris was unhappy at receiving another phone call from her late that evening but he promised a return visit. The next day he found her concerned about the presence of the face and her privacy. He examined the door and measured to see if there was 'a discernible warp' as he put it.

'Beats me,' he said, 'I can't see or feel anything up close.'

'You're not suggesting I'm imagining it I hope.'

'No,' he replied soothingly, 'I'm sure you can see it and we'll try to get rid of it.'

'Its most disconcerting, when I look up and catch it watching me, smiling. Its intrusive.'

'You don't ever shut this middle door then.' Indicating the door between lounge and hall.

She quelled him with an acid stare.

More arrangements were made but this time the door would be taken off, sanded primed undercoated and repainted.

The following weekend found the flat draped and shrouded in dustsheets; china packed away and curtains down.

'Really this is most inconvenient.' muttered Miss Simpson as she let Mr. Morris and son in, and herself out.

'Yes it is.' said Mr. Morris under his breath.

His son looked at the door.

'What's wrong with it then? Looks a good enough job to me.'

'Blowed if I know but she says she can see a face, and she's paying. As long as she pays I'll paint.'

'Must have more money than sense.'

'Well she's got a good job in a bank so she's not short of a few bob.'

'Bet she keeps her money under the bed.'

'Funny you should say that...'

Both men laughed and started work.

After her weekend away in a less than adequate hotel Miss Simpson was looking forward to returning to the sanctity of her home, but on opening the door had an inexplicable feeling that someone or something was in the flat. She checked door and window locks and they were secure but could not rid herself of the sense of intrusion. She ran her fingers over treasured pieces of china, plumped pillows and comforted herself with a hot cup of tea, but still the nagging doubts persisted.

Later as she sat reading, her attention wandered time and time again to the door, but the face did not return. Now the crisis had been averted she craved a little of the excitement of the past week, even though it had inconvenienced her.

Early the next morning with coffee in hand she hurried into the hall to pick up her mail and she saw the face appear slowly and look into her eyes as she straightened up. The coffee made a rapidly widening stain and she stared in shock as the smiling face enlarged into a head and shoulders. It seemed to be mocking her.

She phoned Mr. Morris immediately who felt he had adequately fulfilled his contract especially as she refused to pay, and he ended by quoting an astronomical sum for future work. Miss Simpson hung up.

Later in the staff room over her sandwiches she read a magazine article about a similar problem. A woman had been troubled by the reflection from a window and placed a screen between the window and her eye-line. Eminently sensible, thought Miss Simpson and purchased a large Victorian jardinière later that day. She struggled homeward with it in a taxi, placing it in the hall between the door and the lounge. This somewhat allayed her thoughts of intrusion and she made a conscious effort to avoid looking at the door as she passed.

The next few weeks passed in a blur as new technology caught up with the bank there was much to learn mastering the new computer system and she became more and more harassed by her new workload.

She saw the face reappear many times and it grew a body legs and arms, but now she could not be startled by it and quite enjoyed its appearance in her solitary existence. She scolded herself one morning when she discovered she was talking to the face as she prepared her breakfast, but still said 'bye love' when she left for the office.

Going home became even more delightful and she entered her flat with a cheery hello on her lips. Over supper she regurgitated the trivia of the day to the enthralled face of love as she now called him, without even noticing the face had acquired a gender. She gossiped throughout the evening laid bare her innermost thoughts and private fears and desires.

 Over the next months she talked as she had never talked before and released from the prison of her own neurosis she bloomed. She never seriously thought love would reply although secretly wished he would and was elated when she heard his first softly whispered word of encouragement. After her years of loneliness his presence was like a breath of spring, a long awaited companion, never overstepping the bounds of propriety and respecting her modesty.

 One night as she prepared the evening meal she

felt the lightest of touches on her shoulder and turning knew she would find him standing there.

'My love.' She whispered as she moved into his arms.

Younger women at the bank noticed the more feminine touches, the faint smell of perfume, the hint of lipstick, the modern hairstyle, and gossip and intrigue rumoured there was a love in her life. If Miss Simpson heard she made no comment but lowered her eyes to her work that she now found easier as she relaxed. Now she enjoyed her work and made innovations she would not have dared to before. But as she ploughed through the increasing loads of file and documents she found herself waiting breathlessly for the end of the working day.

Meals became the highlight of her evening and she planned them meticulously. The local butcher and grocer marvelled that she was 'fixed up' as they put it. She had to be she was buying for two now. She bought new clothes, her taste in music expanded and with someone to discuss topical issues, her horizons broadened. Returning home to love became the focus of her life.

One morning she went to see her line manager and handed in one month's notice. He was worried for her, he had noticed a change in her, how would she manage, but she reassured him she would be fine. She was leaving to get married and her fiancé would support her as they intended to start a family right away.

At last her final day arrived and her new -found popularity meant she was invited to a farewell lunch at a local wine bar. Here, her colleagues presented her with a wedding present, a state of the art coffee maker. She countered their questions with her story about a wealthy suitor and showed them magazine pictures of her chosen wedding gown. For the first time in her working life, she was one of the girls and having fun. She was ecstatic.

An inebriated Miss Simpson was given the afternoon off and she returned home earlier than usual, juggling her briefcase and the boxed coffee maker and giggling as she repeatedly dropped her house keys.

She finally stepped into her hallway, the 'I'm home love,' frozen on her lips as a rough hand covered her mouth and whispered gruffly,

'Don't make a sound and you'll be all right.'

Brutally strong arms marched her into the lounge and pushed her roughly on to the sofa.

'Please don't hurt me.' she cried.

The man laughed. He was big and bulky wearing a ski mask, motor bike leathers and gloves, and he terrified her. He was an alien being in her inner sanctum.

'Where do you keep your money?' he snarled, 'I've looked everywhere.'

She shook her head and trembled.

'Look lady I don't want to get rough just tell me where you keep the money.'

Finally he sensed she had nothing to say and he grabbed her throat with both hands and started to squeeze. Suffocating in her own blood and dizzy from lack of oxygen she struggled vainly for a few moments but the man was exceptionally strong and had her pinned beneath him. Her ragged breathing slowed and she started to lose consciousness. Then she heard an inhuman snarl of rage and suddenly the man's weight was lifted from her. She gasped, inhaling air into her tortured lungs and oblivious of the pain struggled to sit upright. She couldn't see the man but could hear fighting mixed with unearthly screams and a sudden snap. The last thing she did see before she blacked out was the tender loving face of her love.

Two ambulances sped away into the night, one carrying the battered and bloodied body of the unconscious barely live Miss Simpson. The other carrying the dead body of the young burglar found mangled in the wreckage of the flat.
DI Winter shook his head as he approached the police surgeon.
'Any ideas?'
'No. How the hell she fought him off I'll never know.'
'Want to hazard a guess to the cause of death?'
'Off the record a broken neck, that seems to be his blood all over the walls and someone bounced him off them like a rag doll. She didn't have the strength to lift him that high and inflict those injuries. No

other suspects?'

'There was nobody else involved. A neighbour phoned the police when he heard her scream and then stayed where he could see the door. No one went in or out. When we arrived we had to break the door down.'

'Any idea who the lad was?'

'Yes, David Morris. He decorated the flat with his Dad a few months ago probably had a key cut then, no sign of forced entry. He let himself in couldn't find what he wanted, amused himself by trashing the place and waited for her to come home.'

'Poor woman.'

'Scum like David Morris, deserve everything they get but he didn't bargain for this. How did such a little woman fight off such a brute?'

DI Winter surveyed the havoc around him and shook his head.

'Perhaps we'll never know the real truth but what ever caused his death wasn't taking any prisoners.'

The forensic team worked long and hard for many hours and after they departed DI Winter closed the door of the flat and repositioned the crime scene tape.

On the other side of the door, love waited for Miss Simpson to return.

MEETING THE DUKE

Dolly lay on the floor watching the kitchen clock tick minutes away. She dared not move, for with each exploratory stretch a searing pain engulfed her, threatening unconsciousness. Uncontrollable shivering coursed through her frozen limbs heightening the pain in her side. She had tripped on the stairs and lain all night on the stone floor getting colder and more frightened as each hour dragged past, but if she stayed alert for another fifteen minutes the paperboy would arrive with her one daily luxury and discover her, she hoped.

He wasn't her ideal paperboy with a shaven head, studs in his nose and lips and many earrings all in one ear. On his first day he stealthily slipped round to the back door before she had burst through and flown at him with her broom chasing him back to the front of the house.

He stood his ground on the gravel path trying to explain then thrown back his head and laughed at her! In the middle of his tongue there was another huge stud. She had screamed at him, called him pervert, craven and any other adjectives that had sprung to mind. At the gate he had thrown her paper at her feet and pedalled off on his bike calling her a daft old bat.

That day had started her vendetta to get him replaced. Every day he delivered the paper on time, every week her bill and change correct, but she was convinced he would steal anything he could lay his hands on. He had his own phone, and what did he want that for unless he was up to no good.

Every morning she chased him and every morning he laughed and called her a silly old bat. At the gate he taunted her as she threatened him with her broom, retribution and the sack. He just smiled showing a mouth of silver teeth, and said, 'The hell you will.'

She hired a taxi to town, marched into the newsagent and demanded that he be sacked. Mr. Fellows was most unhelpful.

'Miss Potter if he hasn't stolen anything why should I sack him?'

'Because he might one day, he lives on the council estate.'

'But that's no reason to condemn the lad out of hand.'

'Anyone who dresses like a heathen doesn't deserve a job.'

'They may not be our ways, but the lad's dress sense and where he lives doesn't preclude him from doing the job. They all look the same now.'

Eventually she had retired, her dignity badly shaken, and retreated homeward.

The following morning the boy had been sullen but obdurate, parking his bike on her lawn while he confronted her.

'I'm not trying to rob you. Don't try and get me the sack again or I'll send my Dad round.'

He had slapped the paper into her hands and sauntered down the path whistling as if he owned the world.

Over the next few weeks he became progressively bolder and she had to keep her wits about her to prevent him intruding further into her domain.

Now as she waited for the whoosh of his bike on the gravel she prayed he would realise when she didn't chase him, something was wrong. There was no one else she thought. Over the years she had rebuked all neighbourly good intentions, even the Vicar stopped calling. She didn't take milk, bills were paid via the bank and she had no family. If she couldn't make the boy hear then she would lay here forever. Her cottage was way back off the road and she was known to repel all visitors.

What was his name and supposing he heard her call out but refused to help? He had no reason to, all she had ever done was accuse him of stealing. She blushed with embarrassment as she remembered the second episode with Mr. Fellows.

'I gave him five pounds and he has not returned my change.' She said indignantly.

'Are you sure Miss Potter?'

'Definitely.'

'I find it hard to believe, people are always telling me how honest he is.'

Mr. Fellows reluctantly gave the money to her. She left triumphant, but when she returned home, she found an envelope with her change and a note of explanation and an apology.

She, had never apologised to the boy or Mr. Fellows, or returned the money.

Suddenly she heard his tyres crunching to a halt on the gravel and his footsteps coming nearer. He hesitated at the front door and then the plop of the paper on the mat.

Summoning all her strength she croaked

'Boy, boy.'

Her throat was dry from pain and fear her voice barely rose above a whisper. The only sound she could hear was her heart pounding in her chest. Had he gone?

'Boy, boy!' she cried with greater urgency, but could still hear nothing.

Please let him realise and come to the back door. Her heart jumped as with startling clarity she remembered locking the stout back door last night.

Struggling to catch any sound, she thought she heard his footsteps going round the house. Was it her imagination? She held her breath ready to call again. She hadn't heard his bike on the gravel so maybe he was still there.

The catch on the back door rattled and a voice called out,

'Miss Potter?'

'Boy! ' She cried.

The only sound she heard was her harsh and rasping breathing.

'Miss Potter! Miss Potter?' louder this time.

'I'm on the floor. I'm hurt. Oh boy, boy!'

Again the silence and then a sharp crack as glass

broke.

Then the boy was there complete with studs and earrings, with a large knife in his hands.

She was right all along, he hadn't come to rescue her but to rob or murder her.

The boy smiled down at her and sheathed the knife before putting it back on a belt loop.

'Now what have you been doing?' He gently lifted her head and placed a cushion under it.

'I fell I think. I don't really know, but I am in a lot of pain.'

'You're very cold, I'll get something to cover you.' And he disappeared. She heard him overhead in her bedroom where no man had ever ventured, and then he reappeared with a blanket and eiderdown.

He covered her, carefully pulling her dress down over her legs. She realised in one humiliating moment she had soiled herself but the boy took no notice.

He removed her wet slippers and rubbed her frozen toes until she could feel warmth in them and in the comfort of the covers she began to feel drowsy.

The boy hovered over her and gently brushed her lips with a damp cloth. She sucked at the moisture eagerly.

'Miss Potter can you hear me? I can't give you anything to drink because you may need an operation. I think you may have broken your hip. We did this at first aid last week.'

'Did you boy?' she whispered.

He moistened her lips again.

'My name is Wayne.'

'As in John?' she queried with a faint smile.

'That's it Miss P. as in John.'

Now his daily taunt of, 'The hell you will!' made sense.

No male had ever called her by her christian name only her father.

'My name is Dolly.'

'Nice to meet you Dolly.'

He dialled a number on his mobile phone speaking softly but authoritatively of injuries and directions to her home.

'The ambulance is on its way. I'll stay with you until they come and then I'll lock up for you. Don't you worry about a thing my Dad will mend the window. He's a joiner.'

She smiled and sank further into the warmth and comfort of the covers.

'Try not to go to sleep.' He spoke softly to her. 'The paramedics will need to know about your accident and stuff.'

He held her hand sitting beside her, oblivious of the mess on the floor, quietly talking and stroking her face.

He told her about his Dad, an old movie buff, his surname Johns, and how he was highly tickled to have a son and name him Wayne after 'The Duke'. About his Mum, a school dinner lady by day and an amateur opera singer by night, and how if his O's and A's were good enough he wanted to be a doctor some day.

She listened to him and as the wail of the ambulance drew nearer she said

'Well Wayne Johns, you are my hero, even if you're name is back to front.'

She closed her eyes and heard him murmur silly old bat.

It was the most wonderful term of endearment she had ever heard.

ONE GOOD SEED DESERVES ANOTHER.

Charlotte Ash returned home from her husband's funeral, alone but well satisfied, everything had worked out so well. The beautiful floral tributes from Arthur's many gardening friends had lined the church with colour. The sermon was short but emotive, the hymns traditional and uplifting. The weather was perfect, dry and balmy with a light breeze drifting over the cemetery. Yes, she thought, Arthur's funeral had been as perfect as their life together.

Charlotte stood for a few moments in the pristine hallway drinking in the stillness. How she'd scrubbed and polished after Arthur's death, anything to keep her mind off his dying. Now the worst was over the funeral signalling the start of her new life in her home where no one would be allowed to invade.

Arthur had tried in the early years with his little sorties into the social whirl of suburbia.

'Shall we have John and Alice over for drinks this evening?' he'd said.

'Shall we invite Bob and Vera for dinner?'

Charlotte had made the house rules very clear.

'I'm not spending all day cleaning and scrubbing, for you to bring home your drunken friends.'

'I'm not slaving over a hot oven so your friends can

eat for free!'
Soon Arthur ceased to invite colleagues or friends to the house.

Their only moment with pleasures of the flesh had resulted in their daughter Arlene and the resolution by Charlotte that she had done her duty.
Arlene's life was as ordered as Arthur's was.
'Don't wear your shoes in the house, only slippers.' Came the reprimand from Charlotte.
'Don't slouch, don't squint.'
'No, you cannot have a dog, nasty smelly hairy things.'
As Arthur spent longer and longer in his beloved garden Arlene had retreated to her room and a world of books.
Arthur became a much loved figure in his oversized gardening coat, pottering around his prize winning garden, often passing the time with neighbours and passers by until it was too dark to see, and he would retire indoors to listen to Charlotte's ever increasing catalogue of woes.
Arlene closeted in her room with the myriad books bought by Arthur for his adored only daughter, became an excellent scholar and won a first at Oxford, escaping her mother's obsessive ways by taking a job in Canada.
Charlotte had watched her husband and daughter as they strolled in the garden together, talking and laughing, sharing a communion she had excluded herself from, and she waited. Her time would come

she knew with certainty.

Charlotte had ruled her husband and daughter in most things but never could she invade their private worlds.

When Arlene eventually married and settled in the States she had breathed a sigh of relief. She wrote long weekly letters to her father who corresponded equally fervently with love and news of his garden.

He had certainly had green fingers. Whatever plant, bush or tree he touched flourished madly. His floral contributions won annual cups at local and national shows. He was known and respected throughout the gardening fraternity and was often asked to speak on local radio stations as the resident gardening expert.

Charlotte, whilst resenting every moment he gave to his precious garden, none the less basked in his reflected glory as the wife of a minor celebrity.

Of all the symbols of Arthur's happy presence in the world none rankled so much as his old gardening coat. It represented the one bastion in his life that she could not lay siege to.

Twice she packed the coat off to jumble sales only to have some kind soul, having seen Arthur wearing it, return it to him. He profuse in his thanks to the bearer and Charlotte inwardly seething as he pulled the coat on to attend to another spate of weeding.

Once she had thrown the coat onto a bonfire but the leaves and general garden debris had failed to blaze under her ministrations, as they were too damp and the coat had just smouldered a little. Ever after it had smelled of smoke but Arthur thought that added to its charm. It hung on the door of the garden shed and Arthur on returning from work, would don the coat filling its pockets with all kinds of contraband. Sweets for the local children, seeds for neighbours, cuttings for the elderly and housebound. He would bestow these little treasures with a smile and a cheery word while she watched disapprovingly from the kitchen window. On his return his interrogation would begin.

'Who did you talk to?'

'What did you talk about?'

'Was it necessary to spend so long chatting?'

Arthur would smile apologetically but remain silent and it was this inability to needle him that drove Charlotte mad.

Soon Charlotte began to see Arthur as the blot on her landscape, the thorn in her side; the hiccup in her well ordered life. Without him their would be no meals to cook, no socks or underwear to wash, no mud trailed into her immaculate house and time would be her own.

Charlotte sought her own solutions to the problem. Over the last two years she had administered poison several times with no success.

Arthur had never suspected, blaming a virus, or food poisoning, or even indigestion. Their overworked and under-funded GP had dished out the customary advice and placebo prescriptions and Charlotte had ensured the doctor's visits were very regular. When the death certificate was issued the regulation fortnight would be well documented with His continuing ailments.

So this time she had crushed laburnum seeds into Arthur's favourite dish of Shepherds pie, and shortly after consuming this, his last supper, he had collapsed. He had crawled into the hallway retching. Rolling his eyes with every excruciating wave of pain he'd beseeched Charlotte to help him. She had ignored his pleas, which became fainter and fainter. When he had finally stopped vomiting and was sufficiently weakened to offer no resistance, she had dragged him to their bed. Here he had slipped into a coma and died at four in the morning.
She had delayed calling the doctor until nine in the morning when the surgery had opened and had spent the intervening hours cleaning the house, leaving nothing to chance. As Arthur, at Charlotte's insistence, had been treated for chest pains so recently, the doctor signed the death certificate as heart failure without question, and today Arthur had gone to his final resting place or the garden in the sky. Charlotte winced at her attempt at humour and set about making a cup of tea.

A shadow passed the kitchen window and she glanced up and her own heart nearly stopped. For a moment she thought she'd caught a glimpse of

Arthur passing the window or at least that great flapping coat of his. She shook herself mentally not only had she buried Arthur but she had made sure the coat had gone with him. The undertaker had looked shocked when she'd turned up with the dirty smelly coat and requested that her husband be buried wearing it, but his gardening friends had understood.

'How thoughtful. She knows he could not bear to be parted from that coat.' Said one.

'It's as much a part of Arthur as his garden.' said another.

So Arthur had been buried wearing his old gardening coat and Charlotte had breathed a sigh of relief at the double demise

She realised how exhausted she felt, a release of the tension of the past few days perhaps. She decided on an early night and after a few perfunctory tasks, wearily took herself off to bed.

She fell asleep immediately and drifted into a dream, disturbing and nightmarish.

She awoke covered in sweat, her heart thumping madly in her chest. She lay breathing deeply, stilling her fears, remembering what she could of the dream, trying to be aware of what had frightened her so much. She remembered feeling very cold as if caught in a draught of icy chilling air and had turned her head to an open doorway as if expecting someone to come in to the room.

How many times had Arthur done just that she

thought, come in from his precious garden leaving the door wide open, trailing mud into the house, as he enthused about this or that plant?

She turned to look at the clock; it showed four a.m. well it was too late to go back to sleep now. Nothing for it but to get up and start work.

She swung her legs out of the bed and after struggling into her dressing gown made her way downstairs.

On the stairs she stopped, shocked at the scene below, the garden door was open and swinging in the breeze. There was mud thickly caked on the welcome mat and spattering on to the hall carpet.

I've been burgled she thought.

She was sure she had locked the door last night. Security was a ritual with her, milk bottles on the doorstep, doors and windows locked, plugs pulled out and lights switched off. How could she have made a mistake!

Hurrying from room to room, she frantically checked valuables and electrical goods. Everything seemed safe and untouched, her eyes roved wildly round each room cataloguing contents. The only thing out of place was her wedding photograph, glass smashed and laying on the living room floor.

Convinced now she had left the door open due to tiredness and the draught had caught the picture she made a mental note to talk to her immediate neighbours about the mud their cat had quite obviously brought into the house; and so she rationalised the incident.

However several times during the day she felt uneasy and gave a little shudder as if someone had walked over her grave as the saying goes.

She kept seeing something out of the corner of her eye, at the kitchen window, but when she turned towards it and focused there was nothing there.

After tea she stared out of that window looking out into the garden as she'd often done when Arthur was alive. She watched the swinging lilac bushes the bright bobbing blooms of chrysanthemums. The swish of rushes at the edge of the ornamental pond and gazed fondly at her saviour the laburnum tree. Funny how in forty years the tree had been her only contribution to the garden. Bought ten years previously to hide Arthur's compost heap. A rash impulse buy that Arthur had found immensely amusing, as he'd explained it would be years before it grew to maturity and covered the offending heap.

She stiffened. There was someone under the tree. She squinted. Struggling to see clearly against the encroaching twilight. There was someone there! Beneath the laburnum tree, a man was standing. He was watching the house, his hand on the tree trunk, head inclined toward the house. As she stared the man moved stiffly and slowly walked purposely towards the kitchen window.

Something about the man was familiar. The way he walked and swung his arms. Charlotte felt her heart miss a beat as the man approached. She recognised the coat! Arthur's gardening coat and as if mesmerised her eyes slipped upward to the man's face as he neared the house. Charlotte saw the smile, Arthur's smile. It was Arthur---- but it couldn't be!

Frantically she squeezed her eyes shut praying the apparition would be gone when she opened them again. She muttered long forgotten prayers fervently calling upon a little known God to protect her. She stood still for the longest time, hardly daring to breathe, her heart beating wildly until she thought she'd faint. Sick with apprehension and terror she at last had to look. The man was gone.

She made for the drinks cabinet and poured herself a good stiff drink. Teetotal all her life she knocked it back in one and poured herself another, this time sipping primly.

Of course it hadn't been Arthur. How could it be, Arthur was dead, dead and buried in that dreadful coat. It must have been an old tramp, probably looking for a handout.

Later that evening before retiring Charlotte double-checked all the doors, putting on the security locks and anti burglar light above the porch. Finally she locked herself in her bedroom.

She fell into a fitful sleep disturbed by strange images and weird sounds, She awoke again her heart hammering furiously he breathing ragged as she struggled to sit up. She turned on the bedside light, the clock said four a.m. There was a chilling draught and she instinctively pulled the bedclothes around her. Why was she so frightened? What had frightened her?

She turned her head slowly as an automaton would, into the draught. She stared in horror. The bedroom door was open and Arthur stood in the doorway, smiling at her, his old coat billowing around him.

'Arthur?' she gasped.

The apparition smiled, and nodded slowly.

'Is that really you Arthur?'

'Yes dear, it's me.' he said.

'How?' she faltered.

'I don't know the how dear, I just know I'm here.'

'Why?' She whispered.

'I think you know why Charlotte.' he said sadly, 'Did you think I wouldn't know?'

'Know what?'

'Why, that you poisoned me ,of course.'

'Poisoned you?'

'Yes dear with seeds from the laburnum tree.' he said resignedly.

She huddled deeper into the covers.

'What do you want?'

'I want you my dear.' He said and flew across the room onto the bed as Charlotte screamed and tried to move away from him.

He enveloped her within his muddy smoky coat. She struggled for breath, gasping as the folds filled her mouth and nostrils. She beat her hands wildly on his chest.

'Arthur, please.' She entreated him. She begged and pleaded as he once had.

'Arthur plea...'
Arthur just smiled and hugged away until Charlotte was still.

Two months later after neighbours complained of a bad smell the police broke down the door of Laburnum Cottage, forced their way into the master bedroom and found the source of the smell. Charlotte dead in bed from a heart attack her arms cradling Arthur's old gardening coat.
The gardening fraternity, undertaker and police remain baffled as to how the coat found its way into her arms.

MAIDEN OVERS

The day was perfect, ideal conditions, mild with a soft breeze. There was an air of excitement and we ate breakfast quickly and in silence. Mother never understood, and was dismayed that her only daughter showed an interest in such things. We dressed for the occasion, he in immaculately creased white flannels and cable sweater and me in my prettiest floral dress with white cardigan. For Uncle Bill and I the Test Match at Lords was the highlight of a long summer holiday.

Not that we went to Lords, but we acted as if we did. Uncle made two flasks of tea. He cut bread and I buttered with real butter instead of margarine, then ham and tomatoes, cheese and boiled eggs still in shells, all luxuries in these austere days.

He ran a long extension lead through the house and staggering under its weight, the huge Bakelite radio was plugged in and placed on the front garden steps. Mother was less than impressed.

'You'll break your neck on that lead one day.' she said.

Uncle studiously ignored her as he twiddled with knobs to get good reception.

Periodically he would hold a finger up to the wind and say 'ah' knowingly and I would wait for his prognosis.

'Following wind.' he said, 'Good bowling.'

South Africa needed 183 runs to win and England needed a miracle, and I had uttered fervent prayers at my bedside last night for just that.

I carried out plates of goodies wrapped in damp tea towels to keep them fresh. Uncle had brewed his home -made beer in the wash boiler and it ran from the tap, thick, dark and smelling of hops, and was dispensed in all manner of jugs to the small group of men gathering at our house.

On the hour we listened to the weather forecast, praying the rain would keep off for Statham and Trueman to make good their promise that England would thrash the South Africans.

Two utility blankets were thrown over the steps and we duly took our seats, with pomp and ceremony, as if at the real thing. We settled back, and soon the melodic voice of John Arlott welcomed us to the BBC Home Service, and cricket at Lords on the fourth day of the Test Match. Uncle Bill pulled out his pipe and I dutifully cut the black three-twist shag tobacco into acceptable pieces for a smoke. He lit up after much puffing and sucking, and the strong woody smell wafted over the assembly. Uncle produced the shiny red cricket ball, presented to him, when he retired as grounds man of the local cricket club. He rubbed it on his flannels as if limbering up to bowl himself.

The South African batsmen Endean and Tayfield went out to the wicket at 11.30 am. Statham bowled five consecutive maiden overs. It was 12.10 before a run was scored and by 12.30pm South

Africa were 40 for 3.

When they broke for lunch so did we, eating alfresco, the sun beating down on us. One boy brought squash and biscuits, another neighbour a cake and after our lunch break the men sipped their beer quietly and I took a nap.

When afternoon play resumed, heads popped over the gate to get the latest results and a small crowd gathered again on our steps.

South Africa were 78 for 7 and Statham had taken all seven for 31 runs, a magnificent effort, but exhausting.

Now at every ball we stiffened in our seats as John Arlott either raised or dashed our hopes. The light had started to fail at Lords, and we'd felt a few spots of rain, but nothing was going to deter us that day. Uncle Bill and the men put handkerchiefs on their heads and mother brought me a rain hat and the radio was sheltered with an umbrella. Nothing was to interfere with this cliff hanger.

We sat glued to the radio listening for the last few balls. Would we, wouldn't we pull it off? I shifted uneasily on the blanket, and waited with bated breath. Chatter ceased and Uncle puffed with stoicism on his pipe. The next few overs were critical, and we listened as the runs totted up, Mansell and Heine refusing to give up.

The bowler thundered down the pitch, thwack went bat on ball, John Arlott's soothing voice told us no run, and the same for the next four balls. My mouth was dry but the men were lubricating their throats with Uncle's beer: and then the final wicket.

' Wardle is taking a short run up to the wicket, its over arm, a vicious spin as the seam grips the worn wicket, and such power, oh and he's bowled a tremendous ball, and he's clean bowled Mansell. It's all over! Mansell and Heine dismissed for 111!' Even the commentator's voice rose a few decibels in the excitement. England had won by 71 runs.

We all rose as a man, off the steps, shouting and waving things in the air.

Mother came to the door complaining at the noise, but we ignored her. We'd won and that was all that mattered.

Of course there was the after match discussion between the men. I listened, sitting on Uncles lap and nodding wisely but not offering comment. When it became too dark to see, the company departed, and we retired indoors.

We had one more ceremony to perform now that the test match was over.

The ball was oiled with a bottle of linseed from under the sink, and buffed until we could see our faces in it. We each solemnly kissed the ball before it was wrapped in cloth and placed in its wooden box until next year. Mother watched with a bemused expression on her face.

'You've got that girl as daft as you.' But she said it softly and smiled.

THE LIFE OF SARAH

The first time he saw her she was naked. On the train home he had idly looked up from the newspaper he was reading and had seen her for an instant, framed in the window, towel slipping as she reached for the phone.
Every Monday to Friday evening for seven years he looked for her, brief glimpses through the lit windows of her home, a warmth in his cold existence. Every evening regular as clockwork he sat in compartment G, seat One A, a window seat, his back to the engine, at precisely two minutes past seven. The train left Liverpool Street station at five past seven and after five minutes swung into a large bend. Here the train slowed almost to a standstill and had allowed him the brief seconds he coveted watching the woman.

She dressed sedately but fashionably, pretty dresses in the Summer with flowing skirts and trousers in the Winter. Her hair was auburn and he had watched it grow, then be cut short, he hadn't much cared for that, and now it was shoulder length again. He sometimes felt if he reached out, he could touch her hair, run his fingers through the tresses and into the curve of her neck.

It was strange how much he knew about her. She was a creature of habit and celebration. She watched T.V. on Tuesdays and Thursdays. On

Mondays she sat at her computer, glasses perched on the end of her nose, first at a large desk top P.C. and now a laptop. Wednesdays she was getting ready to go out, always putting on a coat and gathering her things together as the train slowed down. Fridays she was eating fish and chips out of the paper, just like he would, purchased on his way to his flat, one medium cod and small chips.

Her Christmas decorations went up on December twenty-first and came down again on January the sixth. Every Winter she grew an amaryllis on her window sill and tended a poinsettia after Christmas that was thrown out as soon as the flowers began to wilt. Every Spring she grew daffodils and crocuses in her window box. She changed her curtains twice a year, heavy red ones, velvet he thought in the Autumn and white floating muslin ones in the Spring. She liked fresh flowers and candles. In the long Winter months he had often seen many candles flickering in her bedroom, and in the Summer fresh flowers on the table.

She liked animals, cats anyway. She had two, a big tabby who slept by the window and a younger smaller more boisterous black and white one.

She liked to read, there was always a stack of books by her bedside table with one readily open.

The train slowed almost to a standstill for fifteen

seconds every night at ten minutes past seven, his window into her world lasted exactly for that length of time. Not much time fifteen seconds a day, seventy five seconds a week, three hundred seconds a month, thirty six hundred seconds a year.

How he longed for those moments, thought about them during his working day, greedily sank into his spot by the window ready to drink in those precious moments.

After a few years he had needed more and with the help of a map had traced her home to one street and one of three blocks of houses backing onto the railway line with no garden in between. He ignored the Victorian tenements, too tall and with the wrong shaped windows, casement sash windows.
Then discounted the next block, which turned out to be a nurses home. He surmised no pets would be allowed. That left a block of sixties flats, right shaped windows, right position, with no garden.

Weekend after weekend one long hot summer four years ago he had prowled the street ,sipping coffee after coffee in a corner cafe. Buying newspapers and magazines he never read from the newsagents, purchasing unwanted and unused items from various shops to pass the time while he searched for her.

Then one Saturday he got lucky. She had walked

slowly along the street laden with shopping and he had crossed the street getting to the door just as she did. From then it had been easy offering to carry the bags while she fumbled with the lock and had followed her to her flat door carrying potatoes, other vegetables and meat from a local butcher he had noticed. He didn't linger as she murmured thanks but had turned and left quickly. She was beautiful! Up close she had the most startling green eyes and a light dusting of freckles.

Once he knew her address it wasn't hard to find out her name on the Electoral list in the local library, and from there to the telephone directory for her telephone number.

Sarah Graham, Flat 16, Maybury Court, William Street , London EC 1 3JJ , 0207 431 8222.
He whispered this mantra every night before he slept, dreaming of their life together and the sweet things he would say to her one day. He allowed himself one treat a year on his birthday. He phoned her, hanging up after her first breathy 'Hello?'
And that had been enough, a face, a voice, a name, an address and fifteen seconds of time every day.

Until last week! On Monday when she was working at her computer, he thought he'd glimpsed a man, she had half turned in her seat, face animated in laughter, and then the train gathered speed and he was past.

He spent a miserable Tuesday, being more incompetent than usual because he could think of nothing else than a man in her flat. That night he was horrified to see the man sitting on her sofa watching T.V. with her.
On Wednesday instead of going out she was letting him in! On Thursday T.V. together again, and on Friday both eating fish and chips at the table.

He had fumed and fretted all weekend. Was this a family member? He wasn't old, so maybe a brother? Cousin? Maybe on holiday?

This week his question had been answered. On Monday night he saw them kiss as lovers framed in the lit window. Her lover! He had stared mesmerised by the scene long after the train had passed it burned into his brain. Her lover! Her lover! Her lover!

He had tried looking away over the next few days but by Friday, the pull was too strong and he weakened. He stared transfixed at the window as the train slowed and approached her flat. He saw the banner hanging in the window.

CONGRATULATIONS JIM AND SARAH ON YOUR ENGAGEMENT.

A brief glimpse of many cards on the mantle shelf

as the train gathered speed. He sat numb and descended the train at his station by rote, walking the short distance to his home like an automaton, not even purchasing his normal Friday supper.

He had never thought she would be like the other girls in his life, when he was younger. Had never imagined she would betray him with another after so long. Had never for one moment thought he would have to treat her the same way as the others. That was why he had kept his distance.

Now sitting at his kitchen table carefully soldering the last wire into place and adjusting the small watch face timer, he aligned the wires under the flap and sealed the padded envelope. He turned it over putting on the correct amount of first class stamps before studiously writing the address.

MISS SARAH GRAHAM

FLAT 16

MAYBURY COURT

WILLIAM STREET

LONDON

EC 1 3JJ.

WALKING ON BROKEN GLASS

Alice crept into the room with murder on her mind and in her heart.

Her small almost skeletal frame ached as the damp seeped into her bones. Her pale face, deep lines etched across it contrasted with eyes rubbed red from tears. It was bitterly cold and she shivered. Her teeth chattered as she fought for composure. She groped for the protection of the wall behind her and straightened to face the man who lay in the centre of the room.

The room shrieked poverty with shabby furniture isolated amongst the detritus of newspapers, beer cans and overflowing ashtrays. It was late afternoon and weak winter sunshine struggled through thin curtains nailed at the window, throwing the room into a sinister twilight zone.

He lay stretched full length on a worn couch; his arms folded across his body like a corpse, his beer belly protruded over a thick leather belt. The large bent buckle bit into his fatty paunch. She knew the razor sharp edges of that buckle and had felt its bite on many occasions. His puffy veined face portrayed an air of drunken abandon; his lips slopped open and a thin line of spittle dropped from his mouth to his chin. His obnoxious body odour and foetid alcoholic breath permeated the room adding to other household smells. His head, sprouting grey tufts of hair at irregular intervals, a legacy of Alopecia, added to his grotesque appearance. His feet hung off the end of the couch; toes poked through the holes in his socks and strangled them into obscene fat sausages. She glanced at his meaty fists; his nails encrusted with ancient grime mixed with her blood. She was afraid to look too long for fear they would leap into pounding action against her own frail flesh, a repeat of the earlier beating.

Even as he slept she felt vulnerable knowing she had to stay vigilant for she could not dodge his feet or fists if he awoke. Now she was older she couldn't feint as quickly as she had in their early days together, when the nightmare was just beginning.
With startling clarity she thought back to their wedding on a warm summers day, nearly thirty years before. The church awash with roses and lily of the valley, their heady smell greeting her when she arrived, picture perfect in her wedding gown and he so handsome in his borrowed suit. The excitement and good wishes of her friends and relatives and then her father's impassioned plea for her not to go through with it. Her shock and amazement that her father could not understand her love for this man. They made their vows to stay together and fulfil their hopes and dreams amidst tears at leaving her loving family. These tears turning to despair with the realisation the hopes and dreams were hers, the arguments rage and torture his contributions to the marriage. She had felt so

humiliated that it all went wrong so quickly and she was too proud to turn back to her family, confirming their worst fears.

Today as ever the conflict had started simply enough. The breakfast she'd cooked had been the same as always, but today the bacon wasn't to his taste. She had seen the smirk on his face, the hint of amusement at her haplessness and she'd straightened her back, biting her lip, resolving not to fall into the trap of answering back. He'd sneered and badgered her incessantly with barrack room taunts. Her continued silence fuelled his rage like a malignant growth and soon belligerent words were not enough, and he had systematically punched and kicked her. She curled into a foetal ball and protected her face but submission was never enough and the violence rained down upon her until she lost control of her bladder and urinated on the floor. He'd left her and hurled obscenities as he smashed his way through their meagre possessions. His snores deepened as she waited and watched. Maybe now was her chance.

She shivered again and pulled her cardigan tightly around her. She looked longingly at the fireplace but if she lit the fire too soon another argument would ensue. Her foot touched a brick resting on the hearth and she picked it up caressing its rough edges between her nail bitten hands and hefted it from hand to hand weighing it silently in her mind. A broken nail caught on the roughened surface and it started to bleed again. Could this kill a man? Would this stone break bone and sinew? In his hand undoubtedly, but in hers? What if she didn't kill him outright and he was only stunned what horror would he inflict then?

She remembered the night he threatened her with this brick, his six foot frame towered over her and laughed at her terror as she'd cringed before him. She shuddered still feeling the whoosh of air as he brought the brick down to within an inch of her face again and again. She had prayed for him to use it, to spatter her brains on the wall and put her out of her misery, instead of slowly driving her insane with the fear and anticipation. He kept the brick on the hearth like some macabre trophy, just in case she stepped out of line he said. She put her bloody finger in her mouth and tasted the familiar coppery saltiness and put the brick back, defeated. She didn't have the strength or leverage to batter him.
She stepped over an upturned chair and crunched broken glass underfoot. A table balanced precariously on three legs, she found the other leg its broken shank ending in a sharp splintered point. She bent cautiously and retrieved it, then stood over the man. She held the leg aloft with two hands, as a vampire slayer with a stake over the heart of the monster. Several minutes passed as she willed herself to commit the deed, to plunge the stake deep into his chest and twist with all her might.

'Do it! Do it!' a voice whispered in her head.

She thought of the endless nights she'd lain in bed trembling with terror, anticipating the evil of the rapes to come. Heart pounding as she strained to hear his key in the lock, forcing her mind to go blank when she did because oblivion was infinitely better than the abhorrent indignities she would be made to perform in their bed.

She put the chair leg down and looked at the man, this was no good she didn't have the stomach for it. His death would have to be bloodless. Maybe a plastic bag as he slept, she could pull it tight round his neck. How long did it take some one to suffocate? How hard would he struggle? She put the chair leg down.

After all this time, after all the horrors and heartbreak, here she was standing in the same room planning his cold calculated murder. Contemplation wouldn't finish the deed and she felt a surge of anger at her own impotence. All her life she had shown nothing but love for her fellow human beings and now she was driven to commit the act of murder. This man was more inhuman than human. How could he be human and inflict the humiliations, the defeats, the terrible bone crunching beatings she'd suffered? Over the years she'd got used to the broken limbs, the bruises and lacerations, the lies told at hospitals. The knowing looks from doctors, as they gently probed her wounds removing dirt and glass. They had begged for her to admit the truth and start criminal proceedings. She had stubbornly refused, and endured the long days of incarceration, hiding from prying neighbours whose only crime was concern for her.

Why had she stayed? It was different when the children had been at home; they were the excuse not to leave, even though she knew now staying had done irreparable harm to them. Both James and John were selfish bullies within their own loveless and childless marriages. Thomas could not form a lasting relationship and was in and out of prison with frightening regularity, each crime progressively worse. Even Maria, the youngest and apple of her eye was not unscathed. She had used her intelligence as an escape from the pen as she called it, and with her degree ran as far as possible from her problem family, and she hadn't stopped running until she reached America. Now the only contact was an occasional letter to her mother and cards at Christmas and birthdays.

Still she stayed no longer loving just enduring. Love had been killed years ago, as the aborted baby had poured from her beaten body onto the kitchen floor. She had felt too old, too tired, and too crushed to carve a new life for herself and she was no longer convinced there was another life to run to. She would have to survive in this one or find a way out. The choice was hers all she needed was the courage. Now there was no excuse, she could run forever if she wanted, and she did want! Yet before this afternoon any violent action would have been unthinkable.

Four weeks before a letter had come offering her escape. Maria was pregnant and had invited Alice to America to help until after the baby was born. When Maria returned to work she could then look after the child as a full time nanny. Maria would pay her airfare to America and she would have her own room, all expenses and a small stipend to live on. Alice's heart had lifted just to know she was wanted and needed. She was thrilled and excited to be given a second chance and live with her daughter and son-in -law and the new baby. Maybe she could get away, if she planned it carefully. She could tidy herself up get a decent haircut, mend some of her less worn clothes. Her life had been one of subterfuge of one kind or another, so hiding the truth from Harry whilst she applied for a passport had been relatively easy once she had set her mind to it. Maria sent her air ticket and all she needed was the precious passport to arrive.

And arrive it did in the afternoon post just as Harry returned from the pub. He took the precious package from the postman and stalked up the path to the house. Alice watched from the window with a sinking heart. He read the address on the package and tore it open. His first reaction had been amusement at her photograph. His face creased into a sneering grin.

'God you're ugly!'

His remark tore into her cutting her deeper than any knife. Would his abuse never end? She flushed and pushed away a stray strand of hair and straightened her collar.

Once she had been pretty and boys had queued to dance with her. She had a fair share of boyfriends, some really good catches, but the impetuousness of youth and love brushed all before it when she met Harry Randall. He swept into her life, the loveable rogue with an edge of excitement that all girls of her age craved. He was tall dark and handsome, well travelled and well heeled compared to the young boys she knew. He had a way with the words and the girls, and the chemistry had led her into a full blown sexual affair within days and then a whirlwind marriage. It lasted until the second night of their honeymoon when he beat her into unconsciousness. She quickly realised within the next few days the reality was entirely opposite. He was broke, a liar, a cheat, a thief and a bully. Subsequent wedding anniversaries became memorable by the beatings given to celebrate.

She was brought back to reality by his next remark.

'What do you need a passport for?'

Her mind raced frantically, should she tell him the truth? Surely he would not refuse his only daughter the help she needed. Maybe he would see the sense and let her go, for a while anyway.

'Maria is pregnant and wants me to visit and take care of her.'

'You, take care of her.' He snorted, 'You couldn't

take care of a pig in a sty.'

'I won't be away long. She needs me to help out.'

'Too right you won't be away long.'

'Its just to help out.' She faltered.

'And what about me and my needs?'

She knew it would be futile to argue and bowed her head in mock submission, a lot now depended on her keeping a cool head and not provoking him in any way.

He flipped through the passport, then pushed it in his back pocket.

'You're not going, do you hear?'

She turned away a slight smile played on her lips.

He shuffled to the couch and lay down, snorting and belching until he found a comfortable position, and drifted into an alcoholic sleep.

Now an hour later she was standing here, listening to his snores and trying to decide if or how he should die. Why did it have to come to this? Why couldn't he be reasonable?

She had to find the strength or her moment would be over, and she would be trapped forever in the hell her life had become. Her bag was packed with the best of her clothes and concealed in the garden shed behind a stack of old paint tins. Her ticket was hidden at the back of the freezer compartment of the fridge. The taxi was coming this evening at seven, she had to check in two hours before take off. All she needed was the passport, and time was against her. Only another three hours, it had to be now.

He stirred, stretched and woke.

She froze waiting for his next command, willing herself to remain calm.

'Tea woman.' He barked.

She ceased dreaming and hardened her resolve. This could be the last cup of tea she made in this house. Come on old girl move your legs.

Alice went to the kitchen with murder on her mind and in her heart and a bottle of sleeping pills tucked safely in her pocket.

WELL DEAD

When Susie set out on her morning walk she had not intended to stray so far or get into trouble. The others never moved far from Mama's side but for her the world was a playground of pleasure and adventure, a world for exploration. It was a hot summer morning and the sounds and smells lured her enticingly further and further away from the farm.

She stalked lazy grasshoppers and chased silver winged dragonflies, flying just above her. She sneezed when pollen got into her nose and frightened a small frog that leapt into the air. She rolled in the dust and skittered on stones. Then running through the long grass as fast as she could, jumping and twisting through the air, Susie met disaster. She didn't see the low wall until it was too late to stop. She leapt as high as she could but from the moment she'd jumped her instincts told her she was in deep trouble. Her legs worked overtime as she furiously tried to back pedal and gain a foothold on the rough stonework. For a moment she teetered on the edge, before plummeting to the bottom of the black hole on the other side.

Susie fell a long, long way and lay for some time on her side badly winded. Then she stretched, and gingerly tested limbs to see if she was badly hurt. Nothing seemed broken but she was very shaken and afraid. The well she'd fallen in was damp and foetid with a smell she was quite unused to. There was no chink of comforting light down here, just impenetrable darkness, and icy coldness.

For many hours she jumped and scrambled up the sheer walls surrounding her but to no avail, she could jump no higher than a few feet and could not hold on long enough to make any progress up the well. The cold was now eating into her and she shivered. She was also very thirsty and explored the slimy floor until she found a small pool of viscous liquid and lapped eagerly with her little pink tongue. Soon she was hungry too and she had never known hunger in her short life and cried for Mama to come and feed her. When Mama didn't come she searched for food herself. Small things slithered about on the floor of the well and there was an unpleasant smell that she became attracted to. She nosed into a soft small mound of material and after awhile she found a cold wet source of rancid food.

Carol Anne ran through the grass bouncing and chasing the new ball Daddy had given her that morning. The grass was sweet smelling and growing tall at this time of year. So tall she could hardly see over it, and sometimes the only sign of her was the big blue ribbon Mommy had tied in her long blonde hair before sending her out to play. Mommy needed to cook and get the house ready for her birthday party. Carol Anne was excited because all her friends were coming and even her Nana and Granddad would be there. They were travelling across the state to be with her today, her fifth birthday.

The road and her house were a long way behind her and she would have to hurry because Mommy would worry if she found her gone. It was naughty to leave the yard but if she was quick Mommy might never know, she was so busy. She was going to see Uncle John and she hoped he'd be in. She'd only visited his house once before, with the Ryan twins, before they went away, nobody said where. Carole Ann was very upset because they never even said goodbye even though they were her best friends. It was Uncle John who became her best friend then and he told her he'd never leave just like that. He often talked to her over the fence when Mommy wasn't around. He was such fun and he loved to play with little girls just like Carol Anne, he told her so. He was never too busy to play with his little princess, but she must keep it a secret and then today he would give her the biggest birthday present.

Carol Anne skipped and bounced the ball, singing little snatches of songs she'd learned at nursery class.

Susie heard Carol Anne coming and she whimpered piteously and after a few minutes when this drew no response she threw back her head and yowled. The sound echoed up the long stone shaft.

Carol Anne heard the cries and following the sound she found the well and laid full length in the grass with her head over the wall, and peered down into the blackness.

Ugh! There was a horrible smell and she was nearly sick.

'Hello, hello.' She shouted.

Susie yowled louder than ever and Carol Anne recognised the sound of a kitten.

'Here Kitty, Kitty. Are you down there? What are you doing down there? Can't you get out?'

Susie heard Carol Ann calling down to her through the darkness and she tried a few tentative jumps, digging her claws into the wall and straining as hard as she could to climb, but she could not gain any ground.

Carol Anne heard her struggles to climb the side of the well. She looked around for anything to help but there was nothing there, only the summer grass and wild flowers. She sat down in the grass and tried to think of a way to help.

She could run back home to Mommy but then she'd get into big trouble for opening the gate and sneaking off alone. What should she do? She remembered Daddy telling her about 911 to call for help. That was good but it meant running all the way back home and Mommy would still be mad at her. Daddy was at work and she wasn't allowed to disturb him. She could run to Uncle John's house, he would have a telephone and could call 911 and she could get her present and invite Uncle John to her party.

Yes that's what she would do, go straight to Uncle

John's house and no talking to strangers. Mommy and Daddy were always warning her about that. Wouldn't they be pleased that she had gone to her friend for help and not just knocked on anyone's door?

With a decision reached she reassured the kitten she would get help and return,

'Kitty, kitty. You just stay still now. Uncle John will call 911 and someone will come and get you out. I promise, you hold on now, I won't be long.'

Carol Anne skipped away and the kitten yowled louder until it was exhausted and laid down to sleep.

That afternoon, long after the emergency services had called off the search of surrounding fields and woods, and friends and neighbours had shouted themselves hoarse calling 'Carol Anne! Carol Anne!' They found no trace of the little girl who had mysteriously disappeared from her back yard that afternoon. Even later Carol Ann's Father and the police kicked down the door of the shack where the other kids said 'Uncle John' lived, and found only her bright new ball. Uncle John had also disappeared and a nationwide search began , but as darkness fell, Susie found a new source of food at the bottom of the well and a bloody blue ribbon to play with, and still nobody came to rescue her.

UNCLE BILL

I never knew why he was called Uncle Bill when his name was Samuel Flowers, or how he came to be living in our house as he was no relation, but these things didn't matter to me. Uncle Bill was friend, mentor and soul mate.

When I was born he was already an old man; eighty-one years separated us yet never caused a generation gap that I noticed. My earliest memory is of being hoisted high onto his shoulders and piggybacked round the room, screaming with delight. He was tall. With a shock of white hair never quite tamed, and piercing blue eyes that never lost their compassion or fun even through later pain.

It was his hand I held tightly at the school gates on my first day at school, his encouraging words I remember as he gently prised my hand loose, promising me he would be there when school was out. My first week at school he sat by the gates with his newspaper and flask so I could see him from the windows. I never appreciated how hard that must have been until my own children went to school and I alternately cried and breathed a sigh of relief at a little freedom.

Brown curling photographs in the album show Uncle Bill and I in holiday mood, outside Selfridges in Oxford Street, laden with packages in contrast to the austere days of rationing. Or hand in hand on the promenade at Blackpool, posing with a monkey on my shoulder, or building mega sand castles complete with flags, moats and drawbridges on the beach at Rhyl. He was ever present in my life.

Born in 1865 his life had been varied and exciting. He had fought in the Boer Wars and the First World War, remembered the first air flights and the sinking of the Titanic. During the Second World War he became an air raid warden and received a medal for gallantry for rescuing buried workmen at the docks. Between these wars he had travelled the world and I never tired of listening to his tales of far off places and the scrapes he got into. What images he conjured for me. The crowded junk filled waterways of Hong Kong, the parched infertile plains of Africa where everyone, black or white struggled to eke out a living. The skyscrapers and subways in downtown New York, the magnificent passenger liners in the harbour, and the colours, smells and architecture of India alongside the abject poverty of the beggars. Each story a minuscule geographic, historic and social comment on the times places and people.

I remember lazy days sat on the stone steps of our house with the wireless lead stretched to its full capacity, so we could listen to the sound of ball on bat as England trounced Australia or New Zealand, or the West Indies. John Arlott's mellow voice informing us of progress and Uncle Bill explaining the finer points of silly mid on, caught in the slips, and bowling a maiden over. Through all of this the smell of his pipe, wafting on the breeze. He smoked three-twist shag a foul looking plait of tobacco, as black as tar but with the most wonderful smell. I tried eating it once and was extremely ill much to his chagrin.

I became a poor imitation of Shirley Temple, after singing and dancing lessons, showing no talent at either, but at concerts Uncle Bill was always there in the first few rows clapping furiously, and smiling fit to bust with pride as I pirouetted precariously around the stage.

He actively encouraged my education with trips to the library and museum, suffered with me as I revised for the eleven plus, and practically took out a full page ad when I passed as one of the youngest in my school.

As he became bedridden in later years we spent many happy hours in his room listening to his favourite radio station the BBC Home Service and mine Radio Luxembourg. He instilled a love of classical music and drama deep in me and I taught him to hand jive to 'Hound Dog', 'All Shook Up' and 'Jailhouse Rock' by Elvis.

He fought with my mother over the cutting of my ringlets as she would have liked me to stay a baby forever, but he understood peer pressure, the need to follow the herd, and the desire to spread my wings.

I suppose it was only natural that he should be my confidante during my first wild crush on a boy, the giddy excitement of a first clandestine date, and the despair as I was unceremoniously dumped for a prettier girl. He dished out handkerchiefs and kept his silence as I bewailed my fate at being the ugliest unloved girl in my grammar school. His treat made me feel the most beautiful girl in the world by paying for me to have trendy clothes and haircut at the ritziest store in town. Then professional photographs taken at a studio and rounded off with a high tea in the most expensive restaurant our town could offer.

When he died at ninety-six I was fifteen years old and even though my heart was broken and I grieved for a long time I could hear him telling me
'Life is too short pet for grief or regrets. You have to take life by the throat and give it a damn good shake so it knows it's been shook.'
Thank you Uncle Bill for being a wonderful companion to a very lonely little girl and teaching me all you knew. Through your eyes I have viewed the world and found it as exciting and breathtaking as you did. You are a hard act to follow.